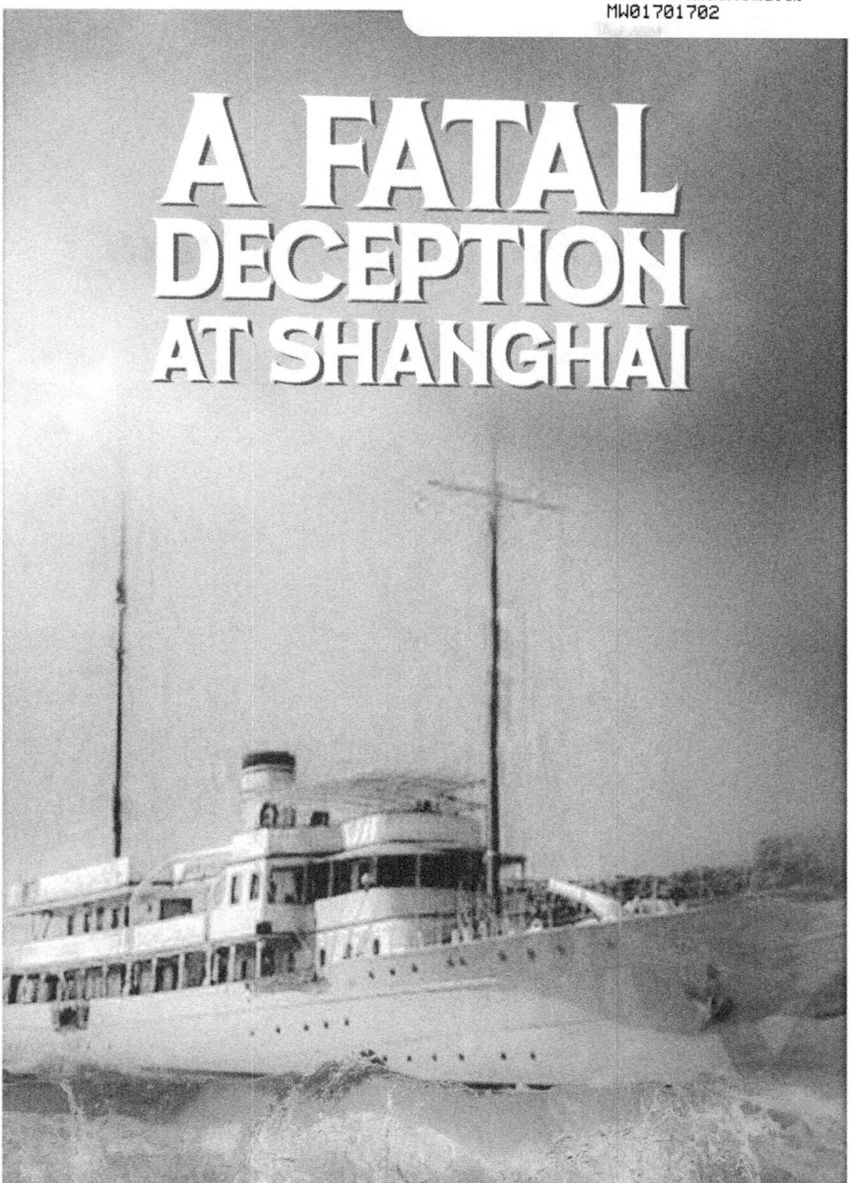
A FATAL
DECEPTION
AT SHANGHAI
Richard D Colbert

A Fatal Deception at Shanghai

Richard D. Colbert

A Fatal Deception at Shanghai

ISBN: 979-8-9862517-9-0

Dedication

To those forgotten souls and survivors who never gave up hope for justice and reconciliation

Acknowledgment

This personal story reflects research and documentation from mixed media, which may include history, public media, and digital archival resources. As such, the author is responsible for the opinions and storyline.

This is a work of fiction. Names, characters, places, and incidents either are products of the author's imagination or are used fictitiously. Any resemblance to actual events or locales or persons, living or dead, is entirely coincidental

Any material/documents retrieved from Internet media resources are within the public domain without copywriting evidence or a clearly visible notice prohibiting their intended use.

CONTENTS

Introduction

What makes the jazz age so fascinating? Is it the glamour and the glitz, the music and the dance, the freedom, and the fun? Or is it the mystery and the danger, the secrets and the lies, the violence, and the crime? This story explores both sides of this captivating era, through the eyes of a group of ex-patriates who find themselves in the middle of a deadly game.

These thoughts draw inspiration from some of the historical events and issues of the jazz age, and escapism from the aftermath of the Great War, the impact of prohibition, the emergence of freedoms, and the influence of social greed. It also draws inspiration from some of the literary works and figures of that period, such as F. Scott Fitzgerald, Ernest Hemingway, Agatha Christie, and others. However, the story is not a historical account or a biographical portrait. It is a work of fiction, a product of imagination. Any resemblance to actual persons, living or dead, or to actual events or places is purely coincidental.

The world recovering from new social change and finds Shanghai as a city of contrasts. It is a hub of international trade and commerce, and expatriates from Europe and America seek new adventures and are drawn to the city's dark secrets. People from diverse backgrounds and perspectives collide and interact in this new age. Life is luxurious in China for ex-pats who live under the protection of the European trade concessions. They have cheap goods, labor and servants to cater to their every need.

During this time Shanghai, was a city, a special place, where anything could happen, and anyone could be someone.

Evelyn Beckmann hated Shanghai. She was bored with everything about this city. Her mother had died when she was a teen debutant, and she missed her gentile guidance. Her schooling had developed one skill that she practiced daily – sketching life as it passed by. Now she had been overshadowed by her aunt, who was old fashioned and sometimes stern.

She had everything she wanted, except for freedom and love.

Her father was Sidney Beckmann, a powerful businessman owned a trading and shipping company. He was also a betting man and a frequent sponsor at the Shanghai Race Club.

She had loved this atmosphere, it was open and green. On weekends she could ride her horse, feeling the wind in her hair. The trade concessions were so pretentious, however there was one exciting escape - International polo. It was more than just a sport. It was spectacle with fast, colorful, and dangerous action.

Polo was a true man's game. Evelyn loved watching the matches, cheering for her favorite players, betting on the outcomes. She admired the skill, speed, and strategy of the game, played on horseback with a wooden mallet and a leather ball. She felt the thrill of the competition, the adrenaline of the action, the glory of the victory. She saw the elegance, passion, pride, and honor of the players, who came from different countries and continents. It was the smell of the dust, sweat, grass, and leather of the field. She heard the thundering hooves, the galloping horses, the swinging mallets, the smashing balls. Polo was her escape from the social boredom and troubles of everyday life. It had become one of her joys and her passion

She often dreamed of leaving Shanghai, of traveling the world, of finding adventure and romance. She dreamed of meeting someone who would sweep her off her feet, someone who would understand her and respect her. Someone who would love her for who she was, not for what she had.

During a trophy match there was a chance meeting and opportunity with someone exceptional. She was thrilled by James L. Sheldon, a young and handsome Army officer from America. He was part of the Army Far East Polo exhibition team that had come to compete with Empire teams in the Far East. He had a smile that could melt hearts and a skill that could win games. He had caught her eye and made her heart skip a beat.

At the end of the match, she had waved shyly, and James took the opportunity to guide his pony to the VIP box and dismounted to take her hand. She gambled a little on his interest and invited him to a dinner at the Astor Hotel, one of the most dazzling places in town. She was nervous and thrilled, wondering if he would come and dance with her, whisper to her, touch her. She hoped he would be the one to make her dreams come true.

The invitation is accepted, however there would be more than expected from this evening. Not the what she imagined. And there was always more to Shanghai than meets the eye. Personal feelings change with the heart and here anything could happen, and nothing was what it seemed. Something here would shatters Evelyn's dreams and James's plans. Was there another hidden agenda, a mystery that offer adventures.

Is it this leisure that makes for excitement and opportunity? They soon discover family and events take a turn. A party on a private yacht is unexpected and they are not alone on board. Not all are invited guests and a stormy cruise evolves into a fight for life, their loves, their dreams, and justice.

Chapter 1

Shanghai, 1926

The world is recovering from the Great War, and Shanghai is a city of contrasts. It is a hub of international trade and commerce, but also a haven for crime and vice. Expatriates seek new adventures and at times seek the city's dark secrets. People from diverse backgrounds and perspectives collide and interact in this new age.

It was as if a terrific draft of wind picked up these very peculiar people and dropped them off in a different lifestyle.

Asia, Europe, and the rest of the world began seeing a large population of these American expatriates. "... the younger and footloose intellectuals went streaming up the longest gangplank in the world." Along with the intellectuals went the wealthy élite, the recent college graduates, the art students, and the recent war veterans. They were the “Lost Generation,” as Gertrude Stein called them in 1926. While some went to discover their meaning of existence - others went worldwide looking for economic prosperities.

China’s financial hub and international gateway seemed destined to blossom into the leading global city of the century. Shanghai was reported in the newsprint as the new cultured and cosmopolitan Paris of the East.

Shanghai was seen as the crown jewel of China, a dazzling city of contrasts. Skyscrapers and temples, rickshaws and Rolls-Royces, opium dens and nightclubs. It was the Paris of the East, or so they said. It was a city of contrasts. But “She” was not a paradise. Beneath the glittering surface lurked a dark underworld of the powerful and ruthless. On one side of the Huangpu River, there was the Chinese city, where millions of people lived in crowded and chaotic conditions, struggling to survive amid poverty and oppression. On the other side, there were the foreign concessions, where a privileged minority of Europeans, Americans, Japanese, and others enjoyed a life of luxury and freedom, protected by their own laws and armies.

Any household in China more complex than the "most modest" was the essence of luxury. Service extended to the last detail. For those with more than a betting interest at the racetrack there was the civility of Polo. Completion was reaching an international scale and the US Army team had beaten the British for the first time. Polo was simple enough but depended on experiences horsemen and each maintained a string of ponies. In China, this was a more affordable recreation, however, the reality was local custom which dictated a need, and the chase would not bend – price was not a consideration.

When the evening grew nearer eight and the street darkened after the long, pleasant twilight, one left the comfortable observation post at the club lounge to hurry home to dress. One called out, and the nearest white-gowned attendant rushed forward standing at attention against the wall. Except for the servants and ever-present young bachelors, the club emptied; no one missed the courtesy of a young hostess.

At home, for the evening out, the best dinner clothes were laid out by the staff. The preferred style for respectable men was to wear a white or black mess jacket with black trousers, universally accepted across cultures. A chic little affair that stopped at the waist with a little pointed tail at the back, a cummerbund, or sash, around the waist instead of a vest, and a soft pleated shirt with a soft turn-down collar. It was the most perfect and comfortable outfit imaginable.

It was not so simple to describe what the ladies wore. The house tailors were unique. Outfits used a riot of color, with all the styles of the world to draw from firsthand, with all the beautiful fabrics the Chinese make in addition to those from home. Patient and capable house tailors, right at hand, make dresses and then still more dresses, all at the most astonishingly low cost, taken together. One gave the tailor an illustration from Vogue, an older dress for measures and the material, and in a day or two, she achieved a creditable near-Paris gown. Every day, clothes become more uncomplicated and more versatile in the modern era. Dresses were designed to be worn with accessories. This made each dress suitable for more than one occasion and was an important way of saving money for other luxuries.

Very few foreigners in China spoke Chinese, while their servants always did, except when addressing the foreigner. They generally assume that their native tongue is a safe code, and one hears surprising remarks even in the undertone between the perfect servants attending the table. It was best never to listen, for it was a little startling, for example, when a lady of the dowager type had spoken somewhat testily to a boy, to see him incline very respectfully. The honorable servants paid respect for consideration and disrespect for temper.

Along the waterfront, a crowd of crewmen might be see carrying racing shells down to the water when the club crews set up for rows during training for the international regatta at Henli.

Afterward, these same labors would wipe and groom the boats into perfect condition after each spin. Luxurious yachts were moored against a background of native junks. Local workers might drag a houseboat along the inland canals all through a weekend party, and the guests, as ideally attended had nothing to do but rest. Sunday night, the social scene was quieter after the business week and strenuous nights clubbing.

The exclusive Shanghai Club was the main stay for many sports needs and stood in an imposing, pillared stone building at No. 1, the Bund. Inside beyond its two-story lobby, was the renowned Long Bar. More than one hundred feet of dark, polished mahogany, it was said to be the longest in the world. A bay window in the barroom overlooked the frenzied harbor traffic and became the place to enjoy tiffin (a brunch or tea) during customary midday break. For those with more than a betting interest at the racetrack there was the civility of Polo.

Completion was reaching an international scale and the US Army team had beaten the British for the first time. Polo was simple enough but truly an exciting game dependent on 4 players skilled in horsemanship, team play, knowledge of the game, strategy plus a string of ponies. This was a time when a US Army Polo team defeated the

British for the first time. General Pershing in Washington DC sees this as an opportunity to boost his budget from Congress and sends an exhibition team to compete with Empire teams in the Far East. In Shanghai, the events are well received, and the U.S. officers are invited to lavish parties at the best hotels and dine at the most glamorous restaurants in town.

When in Rome, one had to learn to adapt to the attitude of that contemporary society. They had to quickly acquaint themselves back into the community with visits to the latest plays, books, gossip, and dance steps. This idea was also accurate for Asia. Especially for anyone wishing to remain in the social swim of things. When you might return on a visit to America or England, you must refrain from talking to your friends about the delights and hardships of life in Burma or Uganda.

Also, it was rude to habitually sprinkle social speech with words culled from native languages (a most irritating of habits).

For an Army Officer, China duty was prized and difficult to obtain. The U.S. 15th Infantry “Old China Hands” assignment in

Tientsin was a long-term commitment, but there were consular and sporting opportunities. However, these positions were limited. The officers in favor took priority for assignment and consider it a needed step for future promotion. This prize could only be had by offering excellence or a unique skill. Noted for decorated war experience, a Lieutenant James L. Sheldon had nurtured favors from old Virginia Military Institute (VMI) classmates and used his native horse sense to be appointed to a U.S. Army Polo team. You make opportunity – waiting for choice is a fool’s game. Now the daily duty assignments consisted of playing in Polo exhibitions – hardly work. The social life was the challenging work –often simply a uniform was added as a plus one to balance out a dinner setting or to escort visiting diplomatic ladies to the various evening clubs. Such was a time for the privileged young officer to share a proper lifestyle. Small wonder no matter how full and satisfying the events were (many could be boring at times) there were invites which were a part of life that would never exist again.

The owner of the Racetrack was known to have made an early fortune in the opium trade and then had turned respectable. As courtesy polo players were rewarded with rent-free lodgings in a large and comfortably appointed house in the French Concession. James was a commissioned officer in the American Army, and rated services but had to pay for local help to support his string of horses in China. A sergeant had been assigned (Dick McClearn) to support the team. But even with low local wages, the need to keep up the elaborate rituals of domestic life in Shanghai dedicated other funding and opportunities were encouraged and expected.

Sergeant Dick McClearn, or "Mac" as he preferred, was a farrier in the 15th Cavalry. He knew everything about horses, from their diseases to their births. He was a hoof-expert in the truest sense of the word. He was also like a big brother to the Lieutenant. After the horrors of combat, he always looked out for him in life. This brotherhood was kept profession however, he was never treated as inferior or less intelligent. He was wise and calm, unlike some with youthful ego. He was also a master of charm and romance. Mac could woo any woman he wanted, from the lovely Romanoff princesses to the former ballerinas of the Czarist Court. In a brief time, the story was this rogue became the most eligible bachelor in the Far East, and many women sought his company.

The individual soldier might pause to recall some things he disliked about his service in China, it was not wholly without its advantages. The Can-Do soldier had been relieved of all fatigue duty and labor to give time to his profession of soldiering. It is said that the soldier in China gained more experience and learned more in two years than in five in some other regiments of the Army. Also, they were offered inexpensive conveniences, admittance to theatres, boxing matches and other performances, inexpensive trading with tailors, shoemakers, photographers, and merchants. Finally, it offered the best of liquors at little cost during a time of prohibition in the states.

Lieutenant Sheldon's major business location beyond social requirements was looking after his Polo equipment and exercising his horse string. Just outside the main artery west of the Bund supplied direct access to the racecourse. Daily amateur jockeys, young tea traders, and bankers would stage horse races with speedy Manchurian ponies. During race week locals and foreigners alike would close down for the events in the spring and fall. Betting was a way of life and many a fortune was made and lost.

It was in this cosmopolitan atmosphere that people meet, and events sometimes disrupt family and ambition that change lives forever.

Chapter 2

The large luxurious hotels—like the Cathay--took pride in the quality of their European cuisine. The finest table in Shanghai was the French Club. Clubs where the hub of our social life and there were, it seemed, an infinite number of them centered on nationalities, sports, professions, hobbies, and any number of indeterminate interests. Most were exclusive, but expected cross-membership and much reciprocal entertaining.

In the blush of the afternoon on a day in the spring, Miss Evelyn Beckmann sat in the quaintly airy dining-room of the Astor House Hotel, demurely sketching a man's profile on the back of a menu card.

Evelyn Beckmann was just nineteen. She was small, quick to feel and think, dark rather than light (though not an out-and-out brunette). She was distinctly pretty. Her small head with its fine and abundant hair, round face with its ever-ready smile, alert brown eyes and curiously strong little chin expressed, as did her slim quick body, a personality of considerable sprightly vigor and of a charm that could act on certain other sorts of personalities, particularly of the opposite sex, with positive, telling effect.

The man, her unconscious model, lounged comfortably alone by one of the swinging windows. He had finished his luncheon, pushed away his coffee cup, lighted a cigarette, and settled back to gaze out at the street traffic. green grasses and diminutive trees bore pleasant evidence that the early warm day of springtime was at hand. Evelyn could see, looking up past the man, the sky lights offering a lovely surreal atmosphere all a foam with color. This brought a thrill that was almost poignant. It was curious, at home—or rather, back in the States—there was little to compare to the privilege taken for granted here. Life was pleasing with so much more said about opportunity here.

The man's head was long and well modeled, with a rugged long face, reflective eyes, somewhat bony nose, and a wide mouth that was, on the whole, attractive. Both upper lip and chin were dean shaven. The eyebrows were rather heavy; the hair was thick and straight, slanting down across a broad forehead. She decided, as she sketched it in with easy sure strokes of a stubby pencil, that he must have quite a time every morning brushing that hair down into place.

He had appeared, a few days back just off a ship from San Francisco. Evelyn had noticed he had walked and eaten alone, austerely. and, naturally, had been whispered about. He was,

Evelyn knew, someone of reputation. The name was Grey Ebbhart. He wore an outing suit, with knickerbockers; he was, in bearing, as in costume, severely conspicuous. You thought of him as a man of odd attainment. He had been in many interesting corners of the world; had known danger and privation. One of his books was were in the British library. She had already taken it out and secreted in her "chambre chic." The literary work was called "Tomorrow in Siam," and proved rather hard to read, with charts, diagrams, and pages of figures.

The sketch was almost done; all but the nose. When you studied that nose in detail it seemed a little too long and strong, and—well, knobby—to be as attractive as it actually was. There would be a trick in drawing it; a shadow or two, a suggestive touch of the pencil; not so many real knobs. In the dining room, she had his profile across an aisle. There would be chances to study it.

Evelyn had been accompanied by an elderly aunt – the proper Mrs. Edward Jason. Her "Auntie" sighed over her idle obsession.

She would have liked to know what this journey was all about. Auntie had concluded that Evelyn had been left just a year or so too long in the States. They weren't serious over there, in the matter of training girls for the sober work of life. Prosperity, luxury, were telling on the younger generations. No longer were they guarded from dangerously free thinking. They read, heard, saw everything; apparently knew everything. They read openly, of a Sunday, books which, a generation earlier, would not have reached their eyes even on a weekday. The church seemed to have lost its hold (though she never spoke aloud of this fact). Respect for tradition and authority had crumbled away. They questioned, weighed everything, these modern children. Mrs. Jason worried a good deal, out in China, about idle young people.

In this woman's good mind there was more real worry. Evelyn was just stepping over the line between girlhood and young womanhood. She was growing more attractive daily. She was anything but fitted to step into the life that lay ahead. Wherever she turned, even now new to the exotic far Pacific—life took on fresh complications. Indeed, Mrs. Jason, pondering the problem, came down on the rather strong word, peril. A young girl—positive in attractiveness, gifted, spirited, motherless (as it happened), trained only to be happy in living—was in something near peril.

One fact which Mrs. Jason's mind had been forced to accept was that most of the complications came from sources or causes with which the girl herself had little consciously to do. She was flatly the sort of person to whom things happened. Even when her eager interest in life and things and men (young and old) was not busy.

In the matter of the rather rude young man in knickerbockers, alone and interesting. Evelyn was to blame, of course. She had set to work to sketch him. Evidently. The most you could say for her on that point was that she would have set just as intently at sketching an old man, or a woman, or a child—or a corner of the room. Mrs. Jason had felt that she must speak to her brother Sidney of the matter. After all, she had that deathly responsibility on her shoulders. Evelyn's only explanation, rather gravely given, had been that she found his nose interesting.

The disturbing point was that something in the way of a situation was sure to develop from the incident. Something Evelyn would advance as a reasonable assumption. And the first complication would arise in some quite unforeseen way. Evelyn wouldn't discuss it. Indeed, she simply had quickly promised not to sketch him anymore.

This is the way it the morning went. At eleven on the following morning Mr. Edward Jason, Auntie and Evelyn were stretched out side by side in their plush chairs, sipping their morning beef tea and looking out at the cities' sea of activity. Beyond Evelyn were three vacant chairs, then this author Grey

Ebbhart —his long person dressed in a fashionable jacket. He too was sipping beef tea and enjoying his solitude - if one considers so dry, so solitary a person could be said to enjoy anything. A notebook lay across his knees.

Mrs. Jason had thought, with a momentary flutter of concern, of moving Evelyn to the other side of husband. But that had seemed foolish. Making too much of it. Evelyn hadn't placed the chairs; the hotel attendants had done that. She had been absorbed in another of her sketching – landscapes with scenes of tropical shores on an island mirrored in the glass of the sea and shadowed against a becalmed junk.

It was time to intervene. She quietly rose and moved to the doorway.

Unshakeable, in the wide doorway, now stood Auntie. Her face wore an anxious expression that had settled, years back, into permanency. The mouth drooped a little. And the brows were lifted, and the forehead grooved with wrinkles suggesting some long habitual straining of the eyes that recent bifocal spectacles were powerless to correct.

"Evelyn!" called the older woman guardedly. "Would you mind, dear... one moment...?"

Her quick, nervous eyes had caught something of the situation.

There was Evelyn and—within easy earshot—a man. The child was unquestionably still sketching.

Evelyn 's eagerly alert young face fell at the sound. She stopped drawing; for a brief instant chewed the stubby pencil; then, quite meekly, rose and walked toward the door.

"Mr. Jason will be waiting outside for us. I think you ought to make plans today, Evelyn."

"No... I didn't know your plans... I was waiting here."

"Well, my dear... it's all right, of course! But I think we'll go now. Mr. Jason thinks you ought to see at least one of the temples. Something typical. And of course, you will want to visit the cloisonné and antique shops, and see the Damascene work. We haven't much time, you see."

But not a word, not a hint, not so much as a telltale look, came from Evelyn.

A chair scraped. Ebbhart had picked up his hat, his notebook, camera, and his unread copy of the North China Herald, and was striding toward her, or toward the door. He would pass directly by, of course, without so much as a mental recognition of her existence.

But on this occasion, as he bore down on her, the eyes of this distinguished man rested for an instant on the table, and for a brief moment he wavered in his stride. He certainly saw the sketch. It lay where she had carelessly tossed it, face up, near the edge of the table. And he certainly recognized it for himself; for his strong facial muscles moved a little. It couldn't have been called a smile;

but those muscles distinctly moved. Then, as coolly as before, he strode on out of the room.

Evelyn 's cheeks turned crimson. A further fact doubtless noted by this irritatingly, even arrogantly composed man. Evelyn, with desperate dignity, put the sketch in her wrist bag, and followed Mrs. Jason out of the building, and stepped into the cab that awaited her.

Chapter 3

The Beckmann family maintained several residences to support business in Hawaii and California, however, in Shanghai accommodations are had at the Astor Hotel and there is the convenience of their yacht in the harbor. The Astor suite is a luxurious and spacious accommodation at the top floor of the hotel. It has a stunning view of the city and the river. Adequate space for a small business office and three private bedrooms for accompany immediate family. The top floor also provides a private salon and dining room for entertaining. Each room is decorated with elegant and tasteful furniture, paintings, and rugs. The hotel staff provides necessary daily services and then everyone has access to the hotel amenities such as the pool, spa, and the restaurant. Successful business does dictate a presence at the more exclusive rooms in the hotel.

Evelyn: (enters the hotel lobby with her Auntie, a busboy follows behind carrying several bags) Whew, that was quite a shopping spree, Auntie. I think we bought half of Shanghai.

Auntie: (laughs) Well, you deserve it, my dear. We need to treat oneself once in a while.

Evelyn: Thank you, Auntie. It was fun to get away for a while today.

Auntie: Me too, Evelyn. You remind me of myself when I was young.

Evelyn: Really? How so?

Auntie: Well, we have the same spirit and curiosity. You're adventurous, independent, and not afraid to try new things and explore unfamiliar places.

Evelyn: Thank you, Auntie.

Auntie: But you also have the same weakness as me. Evelyn: (confused) Weakness? What do you mean?

Auntie: (points to a pencil drawing she had removed from her handbag) Him.

Evelyn: (blushes) Him? Who is he?

Auntie: He's that young author we noticed at this hotel. Aw, it is twice now?

Evelyn: Oh, really? How do you know that?

Auntie: I overheard him talking and he's looking for inspiration inShanghai.

Evelyn: (intrigued) That sounds interesting.

Auntie: Yes, it does. And he's also very handsome and charming.Evelyn: (smiles) Yes, he is.

Auntie: Don't play coy with me, Evelyn. I saw you making eyes at him when we were having tea here this morning.

Evelyn: (embarrassed) Auntie!

Auntie: Don't deny it, Evelyn. I know that look. You're smitten withhim.

Evelyn: (sighs) Okay. Maybe I am a little bit.Auntie: A little bit? More like a lot.

Evelyn: Well, can you blame me? He's attractive, a writer and mysterious.

Auntie: I know, I know. But you have to be careful, Evelyn. Evelyn: Careful? Why?

Auntie: Because writers are not dependable or trustworthy. They'redreamers and liars. Their sweet words make you fall in love, but

they'll break your heart in the end. Evelyn: How do you know that?

Auntie: Because I've been there, Evelyn. I've been in your shoes.Evelyn: (surprised) You have?

Auntie: Yes, I have. When I was young and naive, I fell in love with awriter too. He was handsome, charming, and talented. But he also cheated on me and left me for another woman.

Evelyn: (shocked) Oh, Auntie. I'm so sorry.

Auntie: Don't be, Evelyn. Be sure you don't make the same mistake.Evelyn: But Auntie, maybe he's different.

Auntie: Maybe he is, maybe he isn't. There is always a risk?

Evelyn: (hesitates) I don't know.

Auntie: Think about it, Evelyn. You have a good education and a good family. You might find that good man with adventure, stability, and security. Do you want to throw that away for a fling?

Evelyn: (looks at the writer) But what if he's the one?

Auntie: The one? There's no such thing as the one, some are simplybetter than others.

Evelyn: But how do I know which one is right for me?

Auntie: You don't know, but you have to be smart and careful.
Evelyn: (sighs) I guess you're right, Auntie.

Evelyn: So what should I do now?

Auntie: Well, first of all, stop staring at him. He might notice and getthe wrong idea.

Evelyn: (looks away) Okay.

Auntie: Second of all, let's go upstairs. Your father has asked for afamily evening.

Auntie: And third of all, forget about this guy. He's not worth your time or attention.

Evelyn: Okay.

Auntie: Good girl. Come on, let's go.

Sidney: Evelyn, my dear, I have some exciting news for you.

Evelyn: What is it, father?

Sidney: You have been invited to attend a dinner at the French Clubtomorrow night.

Evelyn: Really? By whom?

Sidney: By none other than Mr. E. Cunningham, the United StatesConsul-General.

Evelyn: (surprised) Mr. Cunningham? The donor of the polo trophy? Sidney: The very same. He's influential and taken a liking to you.

Evelyn: How do you know that?

Sidney: He told me so himself. He saw you at the polo match last weekand was impressed.

Evelyn: (blushes) Oh, father, you're exaggerating.

Sidney: No, he asked me for permission to invite you to dinner. He saidhe needed a favor.

Evelyn: And what did you say?

Sidney: I said yes, of course. It's a great honor and opportunity for you.

Evelyn: But father, you know I am not the diplomatic type.

Sidney: Nonsense. He's a perfect gentleman, powerful, and cultured. A minor event maybe.

Evelyn: Well, I don't know. I'm not sure if I'm ready for anything serious.

Sidney: Don't be silly. You need to settle down with good contacts and insure a comfortable life.

Evelyn: But father, I don't want political convenience. I still have leisure and adventure ahead

Sidney: Trust me, I know from experience. Time fades away, but money and power last forever.

Evelyn: Father, that's cynical and sad.

Sidney: It's realistic and practical. And what's best for you is to accept Mr. Cunningham's invitation and make a good impression on him.

Evelyn: Why? What's in it for you?

Sidney: (hesitates) Nothing, nothing at all. I just want you to be happy.

Evelyn: (suspicious) Really? Or do you have some hidden agenda?

Sidney: (nervous) What do you mean?

Evelyn: I mean, do you have some ulterior motive for pushing me towards Mr. Cunningham? Is it because he's the Consul-General and has connections with the Army?

Sidney: (defensive) What are you implying?

Evelyn: I'm implying that maybe you're hoping to use his influence to recruit some Army polo players to use your racetrack facilities.

Sidney: (angry) How dare you accuse me of such a thing? That's absurd and insulting!

Evelyn: Is it? Or is it true?

Sidney: (calms down) Look, Evelyn, let's not argue about this. It's notimportant. What's important is that you go to the dinner and have an enjoyable time with Mr. Cunningham.

Evelyn: (sighs) Fine, father. I'll go to the dinner. But don't expect meto stand tall and salute.

Sidney: (smiles) Don't worry, my dear. You'll be fine and a simplefavor doesn't hurt.

That evening passes and the unexpected dinner comes all to quickly!

Evelyn: (at the dinner table) This is lovely, Mr. Cunningham.

Cunningham: The pleasure is all mine, Miss Beckmann. You are a charming and delightful companion.

Evelyn: Thank you for your kind words. I'm very fond of polo, you know. I've been following the matches with great interest.

Cunningham: Really? That's wonderful. I'm a huge fan of polo. As you know I am the trophy donor for the Cunningham Polo Challenge.

Evelyn: Oh, how splendid! That's very generous of you.

Cunningham: Well, it's my way of promoting the sport and fostering friendly relations between the international district and trade concessions.

Evelyn: I think that's admirable. Polo is a thrilling and elegant game.

Cunningham: Indeed, it is. And tomorrow's match promises to be a spectacular one. The American team is in top form and the British teamis not to be underestimated.

Evelyn: I can't wait to see it. Who are you rooting for?

Cunningham: Well, as the United States Consul-General, I have to beimpartial. But of course, I have a soft spot for the Americans.

Evelyn: (laughs) I understand. I'm sure they expect your support.

Cunningham: And speaking of support, I have a favor to ask you.

Evelyn: Yes?

Cunningham: Would you do me the honor of presenting the cup to the winners tomorrow?

Evelyn: (surprised) Me? But why me?

Cunningham: Because you are a lovely and gracious lady, with polosense, and ideal as the perfect hostess for the occasion.

Evelyn: (flattered) Oh, Mr. Cunningham, that's exceedingly kind of you. But are you sure?

Cunningham: Absolutely. It would be my pleasure and privilege to have you by my side.

Evelyn: Well, in that case, I accept your invitation. Thank you for this opportunity.

Cunningham: My pleasure. Shall we toast to tomorrow's match?

The evening closes well and a limo is provided to return Evelynto her suite. Her father is waiting; however, she simply smiles, waves,and retires to her room. Saturday will require s special outfit.

On Saturday, the American team claimed the Cunningham Polo Cup. It was quick a thrilling match against a British team played on a well-kept and fast field.

The Americans showed true sportsmanship as they celebrated their victory. Evelyn Beckmann, the gracious hostess, handed the Cup to the winners and received a lovely bouquet from the British Captain.

Mr. E. Cunningham, the United States Consul-General and the donor ofthe trophy, gave a brief and spirited speech that captured the mood of the occasion.

"This country has been making strides in military polo. Last year, when the Americans routed the visiting British officers, many polo fans here and abroad were stunned. The British Army has always produced a steady stream of players for the international fours and to have an unknown American team humble these veterans seemed incredible. This year, a significant effort has been made to assemble the best possible Army team in the country. Players have been recruited from all over the country based on their performance in their division. This has been done not only for the Inter-Army matches but also for the various tournaments in this country. It is the ambition of the United States Army leaders to give this country a representative military polo four."

The Captain of the Army four had been instrumental in scouting for players. His tour of inspection has allowed him to not be satisfied with the material at hand. He has seen the game played at almost all the camps and Army posts. These matches proved to be splendid displays of first-class polo, and he built, it was rumored, this year's team as the strongest.

The Consul waved off the round of applause and commended his countrymen on their remarkable improvement and their ability to compete with the British on equal terms. He also praised the British for their valiant defense and their participation in the event.

Chapter 4

Evelyn was not without attention as well. She caught the eye of Lieutenant James Sheldon, the young horseman and jockey 'at No. 1, who played an amazingly fast and heady game.

Evelyn: (Evelyn sees James walking up to the VIP box. She recognizes him as the player who scored the winning goal. She feels a spark of attraction to him. She smiles and waves at him.) Hello there, handsome. You must be Lieutenant James Sheldon.

James: (James sees Evelyn sitting in the front row, surrounded by admirers. He knows her as the famous socialite who is the daughter of one of the richest and most powerful men in Shanghai. He feels a surge of curiosity about her. He smiles and tips his hat.) Yes, ma'am. That's me. And you must be Miss Evelyn.

She was stunningly beautiful, with long flaxen hair, soft brown eyes, and a captivating smile. She was wearing a red silk dress that matched her red lips.

Evelyn: (Evelyn nods and beckons him to come closer.) That's right, Lieutenant. I'm Evelyn. And I'm extremely impressed by your performance today.

James: (James climbs up the stairs and reaches the box. He looks into her eyes and takes her hand. He feels a jolt of electricity run through him.) Thank you, Miss Evelyn. You're very generous.

Evelyn: (Evelyn pulls him closer and looks into his eyes.) No, thank you, Lieutenant. You're incredibly talented. And very charming.

James: (James blushes and looks away.) You're too kind.

Evelyn: (Evelyn laughs and puts her arm around James' waist. She guides him to the edge of the box. She points to the city skyline, which will soon be lit up by the night lights.) Now, James. I have a question for you.

James: (James looks at her curiously.) A question?

Evelyn: Yes, James. A question. How would you like to dine with me? At the best hotel in town? Tonight?

James: (James' eyes widen.) Dine with you? Tonight?

Evelyn: Yes, James. Dine with me. Tonight.

James: (James hesitates for a moment, then nods.) Yes, Miss. I would be honored. Shall I call for you?

Evelyn: (Evelyn looks at him curiously.) No need just mentioned my name to maître d'hôtel; the staff will bring you to me.

Tom: (Tom smiles and leans closer to Evelyn. He whispers in her ear.) Thank you, Miss Evelyn. You're truly kind and even more beautiful than your reputation.

Evelyn: (Evelyn gasps and looks away. She feels a rush of heat in her face. She tries to act coy.)

The crowd in VIP box is now aware of this intrusion and a tall official looking gentleman steps forward to end the conversation and escort her back to family.

With all the ceremony and formality, Sidney Beckmann had left his box seat area and heads to the stable. His interest is not for the flashy players but it what makes everything possible, the U.S. Army farrier, Dick McClearn.

Sidney: Excuse me, pardon me, coming through. (Sidney makes his way to the stable, ignoring the glances of the other guests and the players. He spots a man in a uniform, holding a horseshoe and a hammer. He approaches him with a grin and wraps an arm around his shoulder.) Hello there, Sergeant!

Dick: (Dick looks startled and tries to free himself from Sidney's grip.) Who are you? What do you want?

Sidney: Oh, don't be shy, my friend. I'm Sidney Beckmann, a proud American and a major fan of polo. And you are Dick McClearn, the U.S. Army farrier, am I right?

Dick: (Dick nods warily.) Yes, that's me. But how do you know my name?

Sidney: I know everything about you, Dick. I know you're the one who takes care of the horses' hooves, who makes sure they're in top shape for the game. I know you're the one who works hard behind the scenes, who doesn't get any recognition or applause. I know you're the real hero of this day.

Dick: (Dick blushes and lowers his eyes.) Well, thank you, sir.

That's kind of you to say.

Sidney: No, thank you, Dick. Thank you for your service to our country and to our sport. You're an inspiration to me and to many others. I came here today to shake your hand and to tell you how much I appreciate what you do.

Dick: (Dick smiles and shakes Sidney's hand.) You're welcome, sir. It's an honor to meet you.

Sidney: The honor is all mine, Dick.

Mr. Beckmann had heavily invested in supporting the racetrack and fielding trained jockeys and healthy horses. Looking around the stables he indicated knew any number of young riders were to be seen riding round the course in the mornings, but what chance do any of them get of becoming good jockeys? They ride their own hacks, or polo ponies, but very seldom are they offered a mount on anything of value. These ponies must have a good feel for the "earth."

How is it, then, possible for them to improve?" Improvement can only be brought about by serious practice, consisting of gallops on good ponies in company with other good ponies ridden by good riders. Surely, therefore, owners, in their own interests, should do more to encourage those youngsters who show keenness and possess a good seat.

Sidney: (Sidney leads Dick to a quiet corner of the stable and lowers his voice.) Dick, can I ask you something?

Dick: Sure, Mr. Beckmann. What is it?

Sidney: You've been working with horses for a long time, right? You know them inside and out. You know how to make them run faster, jump higher, perform better.

Dick: Well, I try my best. It's not easy, you know. Horses are sensitive creatures. They need a lot of care and attention.

Sidney: Of course, of course. And you do an excellent job of that. But tell me, Dick. Have you ever thought of using your skills for something else? Something more… lucrative?

Dick: (Dick raises his eyebrows.) What do you mean?

Sidney: I mean, have you ever considered becoming a trainer?

A coach? A mentor? You have so much experience and knowledge. You could help a lot of young jockeys to improve their riding skills. To learn the feel of their mount at a fast pace. To profit by the example and actions of their companions.

Dick: (Dick smiles and nods.) Well, that sounds interesting. But why are you telling me this?

Sidney: Because I have a proposition for you, Dick. A business partnership, I have a young man of interest, Stevie West, to develop.

Dick: (Dick leans in closer.) Go on.

Sidney: I have connections in the racing industry, Dick. I know people who are looking for talented trainers like you. People who are willing to pay good money for your services and make you rich.

Dick: (Dick's eyes widen.) Rich?

Sidney: Yes, Dick. Rich. All you have to do is say yes to me.

Say yes to this opportunity and it's your future.

Dick: (Dick hesitates for a moment) Well, if this is serious, I have a young officer I have to take care of. We will have a serious conversation. Is that acceptable?

Sidney Beckmann is smiling and nodding agreement. He waves and disappears back toward the crowed stands and his companions.

This Saturday closes with the sun setting and painting the sky in shades of orange and pink. The modern buildings and neon stood out against the horizon, a symbol of the city's history and new culture. The bay was filled with boats of all shapes and sizes, from fishing vessels to cruise ships. Among them, one yacht stood out from the rest, the Golden Eagle. It was a luxurious and elegant yacht, with a sleek design and a bright color. It belonged to a wealthy and influential businessman who owned a shipping company trading with China and other countries. Clearly, the owner has a scheme in mind that will include entertaining guests for a weekend party on this yacht. A captured audience so to speak to insure success and to make some deals.

The night becomes neon bright and festive. The music plays and the champagne flows. The streets were crowded, and the lights were dazzling. Hundreds of people gathered at the Astor Hotel, the most luxurious and glamorous place in town, to celebrate. Daily life just seems to progress in stages.

Evelyn and her young Army Lieutenant are quietly seated at a fine dining table. Her mood has changed and she picks at her food with a silver fork - bored and restless. She glanced around the room, looking for something to entertain her. The music was too loud and too slow for her liking. She sighed and checked her watch. How much longer did she have to endure this?

James was nervous and distracted. He had that conversation with McClearn and his meeting with Mr. Beckmann. He didn't pay attention to what she was saying. He wanted to leave.

He nodded vaguely at whatever she was saying, hoping she wouldn't notice his lack of interest.

(James and Evelyn have just finished their main course, but they have barely touched their food. James tries to make some conversation.)

James: So, Miss Evelyn. How do you like Shanghai?

Evelyn: (Evelyn looks up from her plate and forces a smile.)

Oh, it's lovely, James. Very lovely.

James: (James nods and fiddles with his fork.) Yes, it is. .

Evelyn: (Evelyn clears her throat and looks around.) The hotel is genuinely nice too.

James: (James agrees and looks at his watch.) Yes, it is.

Evelyn: (Evelyn sighs and looks at her glass.) The wine is exceptionally good as well.

James: (James nods and takes a sip.) Yes, exceptionally good.

Evelyn: (Evelyn bites her lip and looks at him.) James…

James: (James looks at her and raises his eyebrows.) Yes, Evelyn?

Evelyn: (Evelyn hesitates and lowers her voice.) James, I'm sorry. I seem to not be myself tonight. .

James: (James looks surprised and shakes his head.) No, Evelyn. Don't be sorry. We all have our days.

Evelyn: (Evelyn smiles sadly and shakes her head.) Yes, I did,
James: (James frowns and leans closer.) What do you mean,

Evelyn: (Evelyn looks away and tears up.) I think I lost someone. Someone I can't get over.

James: (James stands up and reaches for her hand.) Evelyn.

Evelyn: (Evelyn pulls her hand away and grabs her purse.) It's really Ok James. Please stay as my quest and enjoy the evening.

James: (James looks uncomfortable and nods) Evelyn…

Evelyn: (Evelyn turns to leave and speaks softly.) I'm sorry, James you have been pleasant company, but I do have to go.

For James, the night is not going to be a total loss. The bar is open and the earlier conversation with McClearn sounded promising.

He motions to the maître d'hôtel and requests a call be placed to his guest residence at the French concession. Dick would be eager to get out into the night and join him at the restaurant.

Chapter 5

Sunday starts or ends the week in the international corners of Shanghai. For the trade concessions the business community takes Sunday as a day of rest from the late-night dinners and social commitments and expectations. Sidney Beckmann enjoyed mixing business and rarely considered casual time as leisure.

This one early morning finds a small network of horse traders and jockeys working their ponies at the racetrack. The conversation usually turns to business.

Mr. Beckmann greeted Sgt. McClearn and Lt. Sheldon with a smile and a handshake. He led them to his private box away from track stables, where he offered them drinks and snacks. He made small talk with them, complimenting them on their skills as jockeys and polo players and asking them about their lives in the Army. He then got to the point of his meeting.

Mr. Beckmann: Gentlemen, thank you for meeting me here today. I have a proposition for you that I think you'll find interesting.

Sgt. McClearn: We're listening, Mr. Beckmann. What do you have in mind?

Mr. Beckmann: As you know, I own several racehorses and

I'm always looking for new talent to train them. I get the impression you work well as a team and would make excellent trainers for my stable.

Lt. Sheldon: That's very flattering, but we have our duties in the Army. We can't just leave our assignment and join your team.

Mr. Beckmann: Oh, but you can, Lt. Sheldon. You see, I have connections in high places, and I can arrange for you to take a leave of absence from the Army for as long as you need. And Sgt. McClearn, you're close to retirement anyway, aren't you? Why not end your career on a high note and join me in this lucrative venture?

Sgt. McClearn: Well, it sounds tempting, but what exactly are you offering us? What are the terms of this partnership?

Mr. Beckmann: The terms are simple. You will work exclusively for me as trainers and scout jockeys for my horses. You will receive a generous salary and a percentage of the winnings from each race. You will also have access to the best facilities and equipment available.

Lt. Sheldon: And what do you expect from us in return?

Mr. Beckmann: Nothing much, really. Just your loyalty, dedication, and obedience. You will follow my instructions and advice without question. You will not work for any other owner or trainer.

And you will not interfere with my business affairs or personal matters – which includes my daughter.

Sgt. McClearn: That sounds a bit one-sided, Mr. Beckmann.

Mr. Beckmann: Not at all, Sgt. McClearn. Think of it as an excellent opportunity to advance your careers and make a fortune.

Lt. Sheldon: And what if we decline your offer?

Mr. Beckmann: Then I'm afraid you'll miss the chance of a lifetime, Lt. Sheldon.

Sgt. McClearn: Is that a threat, Mr. Beckmann?

Mr. Beckmann: No, no, of course not. Just a friendly warning.

Lt Sheldon: Well, we appreciate your interest in us, but we need some time to think about it.

Mr. Beckmann: Of course, of course. Take all the time you need. You have some days to enjoy a vibrant city with a lot of opportunities and challenges. I do have some important business meetings next week with some of the most powerful and influential people in China.

Gentlemen, lets meet again at the track next Friday evening, after hours, when I will have all the information and documents ready sign. There will be more details for you that I think you'll find interesting.

Sidney Beckmann turns and with a slight wave disappears into a gathering of older men out inspecting a line of horses being led out for exercise.

Sgt McClearn (to Lt Sheldon): What do you think of his offer?

Lt Sheldon (to Sgt McClearn): I don't know what to think.

Sgt McClearn (to Lt Sheldon): Maybe he's hiding something.

Lt Sheldon (to Sgt McClearn): Maybe he is. Maybe he's not.

Sgt McClearn (to Lt Sheldon): I have some real concerns.

Sgt. McClearn: Next Friday evening? I wonder why then?

Life in the Army and some firsthand experiences did set up some warning signs for both of these men. Mr. Beckmann seemed to be a pleasant man, but something was off – all their meetings were more less behind the bar. The remaining hours of the day went without concern and thoughts turned to next week requirements… Another polo exhibition match was on the schedule for the next Saturday.

What was termed as business and social life returned to the international district by mid-day on Monday. Those visiting without commitment spent their day strolling along the Bund, admiring the view of the river and the colonial buildings. There were other distractions with performances by the Shanghai Circus and or a more private visit to the Yuyuan Garden with its garden of rockeries, ponds, and pavilions.

At the Astor Hotel, Evelyn's Auntie resumed her role of interference in everyone's daily life. There was a commotion within the house and personal staff concerning needed preparations for a yacht party the next weekend. The guests would come from a diverse and distinguished group, including military officers, diplomats, politicians, and socialites. They would all have some connection to China and its affairs, either through business, politics, or personal relationships. They also would have some secrets and motives that they hid from each other. So the week passes…

Friday arrives and on board the yacht, accommodations have been made with a short guest list for a private affair. Some early guests mingled and enjoyed themselves.

Among the guests, there was one who did not belong and had arrived hatless, with ruffled hair and a slightly nosey demeanor. He came down the stairs and advanced along the patio deck, eagerly searching the row of recumbent figures in plush chairs. Before the Jason's he stopped with delighted greetings.

It was Ebbhart, San Francisco newsman and author. He had managed to sneak on board with a fake invitation. He hoped to get an exclusive interview with Sidney Beckmann or one of his guests, who were rumored to be involved in some shady dealings in China. He also hoped to get a scoop or a story that would boost his career and reputation.

He showed a sudden interest in a couple and decided to approach. He introduced himself and the exchange was casual, and he responded with charm and wit. They talked about several topics, such as jazz music, art, literature, and travel. They found out that they had a lot in common and that they shared a curiosity about the world.

All this was quite normal for a mixed social group, and he was pretending to be one of the guests, when he saw her. She was the young woman who had caught his eye. Evelyn breezed by and she had that look and those soft brown eyes. She wore a fashionable and elegant dress that showed off her petite and slender figure.

Evelyn was headed directed to the yachts Captain quarters with an attitude visible in each step. Slipping in, without the courtesy of a knock, she spoke up: "Who could have done this gossip?" the socialite asks, clutching her pearls and trembling.

"We're all friends, aren't we?" "Friends?"

The Captain sneers. "Don't make me laugh. We're all strangers here, with our own agendas and our own secrets. And more than one of us is dangerous."

Her father, Sidney leaning against the radio room door, nods sagely. "He's right, you know. We all have something to hide. Something that could make us kill. Or be killed."

Evelyn then frowns. "That's nonsense. There has to be a rational explanation for this. A clue, a motive, a method. Something that will lead us to the truth."

The Captain laughs bitterly. “The truth? Do you think you can handle the truth? The truth is a matter of instincts, my girl. And instincts are dangerous things. They can make you do things you never thought you would do. Things you might regret later.”

Excited whispers had reached her that all on board might be in for a long journey across the Pacific, she hadn't begun so much as to believe the facts. Though there they stood, squarely enough, before her. It had been easier to surrender her responsive, rather easily gratified emotions to a day-by-day enjoyment of life in Shanghai without the constant, worried watchfulness of Mrs. Jason.

This had all reached the point of annoyance—not that Auntie wasn't an old dear; kindness itself, especially if your head ached or you needed a little mothering! —Now this she would be a prisoner for the next weeks without any relief. She decided no one on board deserved her youthful enthusiasm, she would simply busy herself sketching. The top layer of her steamer trunk was nearly full now—sketches of her personal daily life and thoughts

The disturbing point was that something in the way of a situation was sure to develop from a previous incident. In that moment, she had suddenly realized as she had recognized one of the guests up on deck. Evelyn made that a reasonable assumption. And the first complication would arise in some quite unforeseen way. Evelyn wouldn’t bring it about. Indeed, she had long promised not to sketch him anymore. Her efforts would be to ignore his frigid way and concentrate on the beauties of the sea and on the quaint gray distant mist covering images just visible up and down the horizon.

That night, lying in her berth, Evelyn, forgot the present. Her thoughts dwelt among past young friends, the boy-and-girl "crowd," she had left behind, far off, and very softly, she cried herself to sleep.

Chapter 6

A CRASH, and the sound of splintering glass, aroused James L. Sheldon. He sat up, uncertainly, conscious of a dull pain in his head, of a rolling motion and sea air. The darkness, at first impenetrable, shaded sufficiently for him to realize that he was lying on a bed fully clothed and alone in a box-like stateroom. The pelting rain, the rumble of thunder and wind, the pitching and tossing lurches, gave evidence of a violent storm at sea. There was another crash, followed by a resounding bump. The bed seemed to have jerked loose from its floor hooks. Sheldon groped about for a light 'button and found one. A ceiling light illuminated the stateroom, and he was amazed to see that it was luxuriously offered, and larger than he had imagined. He wondered, dismally, what force of circumstance had brought him on board this boat, and what kind of a boat it was?

He tried to recall what had happened in his last conscious moments. His head throbbed miserably, and he lay back on the pillows. Scenes in a night club drifted dizzily into his vision. The Astor House! He had gone there once on an invite from the lovely lady in red and met with some of her family and business acquaintances. They had a quiet dinner and the evening got messy. He recalled, vividly, calling McClearn and spending the rest of the evening in discussion. He could remember nothing further., This incident, however, in no way accounted for his present surroundings.

He didn't have any enemies he knew of none who would be likely to push him off onto a boat, after a crack over the head in a night club. He sat up and his removed tuxedo jacket and vest. The bed slid across the floor with the downward dip of the boat. A faint sense of nausea caused his aching head to whirl dizzily. He slumped back on the pillows. After an interval, his mind cleared again, and he decided to investigate.

He stood up and moved stumblingly about the room. Pulled out the drawers of the dressing-table, desk, and table. They were empty.

Examined the modernly equipped bathroom, and found nothing in the way of identification except towels, with the word "GOLDEN EAGLE" embroidered in gold letters.

From these, he gained a instant impression that he must have been shanghaied on board a private yacht. As far as he knew none of his friends, or acquaintances, owned a yacht.

He pondered over the idea that he had been mistaken for someone else. And jerked open the door of the stateroom. At least, he was not locked in. The freezing wind and the swirling rain made him pause. Angry, choppy waves lashed against the side of the ship.

Foaming spray shot over the railing and plunged onto the deck. Sheldon closed the door, reluctantly. He would wait for daylight to explore further. In turning, he discovered a narrow door opposite, and pulled it open. A long, oblong closet was disclosed, and in the bottom of the closet was a black leather suitcase. He yanked it out, and laid it on the bed.

It was heavy. A white tag fluttered from the handle. There was a name printed on the tag. He sat down on the bed beside the suitcase rubbed his head and stared at the name his own-in utter bewilderment. Then, clumsily, fearfully, he pressed the catch, and flung the top back. Bewilderment increased. The case was filled with neatly packed clothing and other accessories. He picked out a shirt. It was new, and it had his initials in the neckband. He took out a gray tweed coat and tried it on. Looked in the mirror and saw that it fitted as though made for him. No, he decided, quickly, he was not the victim of mistaken identity. Whoever had wanted to shanghai him had made elaborate preparations. He threw the coat and shirt back into the suitcase, bumped it onto the floor; stretched out on the bed. and tried to focus his thoughts on vague possibilities.

His head was pounding, and his mouth was dry. He looked around and saw that he was lying on a narrow bed in a small cabin. He tried to remember what had happened, but his mind was blank. He felt a sudden surge of panic. Where was he? How did he get here? He got up and stumbled to the door. It was now locked. He banged on it and shouted for help. No one answered. He heard a muffled voice from the other side of the wall. It was his sergeant.

“Sir, are you there? Are you all, right?” the sergeant asked.

“Yes, I’m here. Please don’t call me “Sir” This is not the parade ground and my head hurts. I’m fine. Do you know where we are?” James replied.

“Well Lieut. I don’t. I woke up in this cabin just like you. I think we’ve been kidnapped.”

“Kidnapped? By whom? And why?”

“I don’t know, Maybe by some pirates or smugglers. Maybe they want ransom or information.”

"Damn it. We have to get out of here. We have to find a way to contact our consulate."

"Yep, that would be a good start. Time to put our heads together?"

The officer looked around the cabin for anything that could help them escape. He saw a small window above the bed. He climbed on the bed and looked outside. He saw the blue sea and the white waves.

He felt a chill run down his spine. They just might be in serious trouble. None of them seemed logical. He wondered if the crack on the head had affected his brain. He shouted to Dick to stay put for now.

At the first streak of dawn, he ventured on deck. The rain was still coming down in torrents, but the wind had diminished. He was able, by clinging to the cabin rail, to walk unsteadily toward the bow. Seven doors faced the deck. In passing, Sheldon twirled the knob of each without result, until he came to the sixth. The sixth door opened into a comfortably furnished lounge. He was about to enter when his attention was attracted by a faint noise. Atop the forecastle, two brown-skinned men were coiling rope. He went forward and shouted at them. They paid no attention, beyond favoring him with a vacant stare. He climbed down the narrow iron stairway and made his way across the fore deck. The crew were muttering in an unknown language.

"Where is this boat going?" he demanded, as he stood over them. They continued to stare at him. One of them babbled something in an unknown language. The other made numerous gestures, and grunted a little. Sheldon repeated his question, and both men waved their arms, and rattled on in a frantic dialect that, had nothing of the Latin or Anglo- Saxon, Sheldon stamped away, angrily. Looking up his eye detected a man on the bridge. He stumbled up the stairway found the one leading to the bridge, and climbed it. A white mam, uniformed, and smart-looking, was pacing back and forth, leisurely.

Sheldon said to him: '.'Where are we bound for. Captain?" The man glanced at him casually, and mumbled something that sounded like the language that the two brown-skinned men had used.

"Don't tell me that you don't speak English,". Sheldon said, crossly. The man. looked like an American. He was answered by a gesture of seeming incomprehension. He cursed. It was bad enough to be shanghaied but to be at the mercy of a captain and crew who spoke an unheard-of language, was distinctly disconcerting.

He turned away, gloomily, and started to descend the stairway. Part way down, he heard a door open and shut, and hurried down the remaining steps. A stout man in light pajamas was leaning over the rail retching violently. Sheldon hesitated. Between spasms, he thought that he heard the expression "Oh, Lord!" And hesitated no longer. The man might be seasick, but he could speak English.

The man mopped his forehead, pushed back blond, wavy hair, and staggered toward a door. He did not look in Sheldon's direction, and before Sheldon could reach him, the door had closed. A bolt clicked loudly from the inside, as Sheldon stood before the door. He knocked.

There was no response. He waited a minute, cursing under his breath, and then moved on, aimlessly, headed aft. A long drawn-out and peculiar moaning startled him. He paused to sense the direction. Wondered if it had come from the man whom he had just seen, and walked back. Stood before the door again, listening, intently. Noticed that an aluminum "I" lettered the door. Remembered that there was an "F" on the door of the room that he had occupied. A minute passed, and there was no sound. Sheldon thought of knocking again. Then the moan was repeated with an echo of eeriness. It did not come from behind that bolted door, but from somewhere nearer the bow. He walked in that direction.

As he approached the lounge, a voice that sounded repressed and gravely and diminished to a low moan, made him hurry forward. The door was swinging partly open, and the voice droned: "It's murder, murder, murder I tell you “And dwindled to a quivering gasp. Sheldon rushed into the room and saw a 'tall, gaunt, elderly man clad in an old- fashioned, flowing nightshirt bent double holding his stomach, as though writhing in agony. And suddenly, with a cry of stark terror, he toppled overhead first and lay in a grotesque position, at Sheldon s feet.

The man was Sidney Beckmann - the millionaire trader. Sheldon recognized the old man with a sense of horror, as he fell. Sidney Beckmann had been an avid follower of polo and bet heavily on their agreement. Sheldon slowly remembered the meetings and his experiences at the hotel. Now the old man was not making sense.

Beckmann was muttering "Murder, murder " over and over.

Sheldon stooped and caught hold of his wrist, in an effort to feel the pulse, and noticed that the eyes had a filmy, unnatural look. "Mr. Beckmann." he murmured, in frantic appeal, "it's James L. Sheldon. Don't you know me? Tell me what is it? What happened?"

The eyelids fluttered. Sidney Beckmann made a last effort to speak but no words came. Then his head dropped back, limp, Sheldon knew, instantly, that this fellow was dead. He knelt there, stunned, and bewildered unable to comprehend this sudden and awful death unable to imagine details that might have led up to this strange voyage. What was Sidney Beckmann doing on this yacht? Had he been shanghaied, also?

And was he, James L. Sheldon, about to be murdered? He shuddered despairingly. Wondered what had caused Beckmann's death, had he been poisoned? Who was the man whom he had seen on deck? Had that man been poisoned, also? Countless gruesome suspicions shot through his mind. A cold perspiration tingled on his forehead.

Chapter 7

Suddenly, in the background, a voice said, sharply; 'What are you doing?" He looked up and faced a short, slim, dark-haired man, whose somber, brown eyes seemed to be glaring ruthlessly "at him. He had not heard anyone enter the lounge. The tragedy had numbed his brain. The young man repeated the question, waited, and added snappishly: "I suppose you don't speak English, either.", Recollection of earlier ventures that morning brought quick understanding of the other man's thoughts. "I speak English," he returned, swiftly. "You damned well know who I am Lieut. '. "Sergeant Dick McClearn, and I don't know what the deuce I'm doing here. Who is that on the floor? And what is the matter with him?"

The man moved closer, and a look of horror blanched his features, as he caught sight of the glassy eyes. "That's Sidney Beckmann!" he stammered, and rubbed his eyes, as if to be certain of what he saw. "Is he, is he?"

"Yes. He is dead," Sheldon said, quietly.

What happened? Did he have a stroke, or something? And what was he doing on board this infernal tub?" McClearn knelt beside Sheldon, as he talked in excited tones?

I do not think Mr. Beckmann had a stroke. It was something;

else-something, I don't understand. Suppose we go on deck, and discuss the situation."

"Did you find him like this?" McClearn asked, and his eyes narrowed a little, as he regarded Sheldon.

"Sidney, Sidney " a harsh, feminine voice shrilled from the port side. "Where are you?" "Come on." Sheldon whispered, galvanized into sudden activity. "Let's get on deck where we can talk, and clear it was now too late. A tall woman with snow-white hair, wearing a crimson velvet robe, stood poised in the doorway, staring at them. "Who are you? And what are two strange men doing aboard my yacht?" she demanded with chilly indignation. Then her eyes shifted toward the floor, and she saw the still figure of Sidney Beckmann. For a moment, she reeled

Evelyn rushed in just behind the woman... her Auntie Jason

Evelyn: Father? Father, are you in there? She enters the stateroom and gasps.)

Oh, no… Father! (She runs to his side and kneels down. He is lying on the floor, clutching his chest, his face contorted in pain. A glass of wine is spilled on the carpet next to him. She feels for a pulse, but finds none. She starts to cry.) Father, please… please wake up… (She hears footsteps outside and looks up. She sees Mrs. Jason standing in the doorway, looking shocked.)

Mrs. Jason: Evelyn… what happened?

Evelyn: (She wipes her tears and stands up, facing Mrs. Jason with anger and suspicion.) What did you do to him?

Mrs. Jason: What? What are you talking about?

Evelyn: Don't play dumb with me. You hated him. You hated that he was richer and successful, and you weren't.

Mrs. Jason: That's ridiculous. I loved your father. He was my brother.

Evelyn: And you always resented him for it. You always wanted what he had.

Mrs. Jason: That's not true.

Evelyn: Then why did you invite us on this yacht? Why did you give him this wine? Why did you poison him?

Mrs. Jason: I didn't poison him! How dare you accuse me of such a thing?

Evelyn: How dare I? You're a monster!

Mrs. Jason: Evelyn, calm down. You're hysterical. Evelyn: Don't tell me to calm down! You killed him! Mrs. Jason: No, I didn't!

Evelyn: Yes, you did! And I'll prove it! (She picks up the glass of wine and throws it at her Aunt, who dodges it. The glass shatters on the wall behind her. Evelyn runs past her and out of the stateroom.

Grey: Evelyn! Evelyn, wait! (He runs after her and catches up with her on the deck. He sees her face is pale and tear-stained. He puts his hand on her shoulder.) Evelyn, are you okay? What happened?

Evelyn: (She turns to him and sees his concerned expression. She recognizes him instantly as the man she sketched at the hotel and had noticed on board last night. She had tried to flirt in a coy way). Who are you?

Grey: I'm Grey. Grey Ebbhart. We met last night at the party.

Evelyn: Oh, right. We seem to have met before.

Grey: Well, not exactly. I'm actually a reporter.

Evelyn: A reporter? What are you doing here?

Grey: I'm sorry, Evelyn. I just lied to you. I came here to get astory on your father's business.

Evelyn: A story? What kind of story?

Grey: A story about his shipping trade in China. I heard he was involved in some shady deals.

Evelyn: That's not true. My father was an honest man.

Grey: I'm sorry, Evelyn. I didn't mean to offend you. I was just doing my job.

Evelyn: Your job? Your job is to lie and spy and snoop around?

Grey: No, no, it's not like that. I'm a journalist. I report the truth.

Evelyn: The truth? You don't know anything about my father.

Grey: Maybe not. But I know something about you

Evelyn: What do you know about me?

Grey: I know that you're beautiful and smart and brave. And I know that you're in trouble.

Evelyn: Trouble?

Grey: Yes, trouble. You said your father was murdered. Evelyn: He was. He was poisoned by his sister.

Grey: His sister? Mrs. Jason?

Evelyn: Yes, Auntie killed him out of jealousy and greed.

Grey: How do you know that?

Evelyn: I just know. I saw her. She was in his stateroom. She had a motive. She had the means.

Grey: Do you have any proof?

Evelyn: Proof? No, I don't have any proof.

Grey: Evelyn, listen to me. You can't accuse someone of murder without proof. You need evidence. There are others on this yacht who are not family. Let's get everyone together.

Evelyn: I told you, she had a motive. She hated him.Grey: That's not enough, Evelyn.

Evelyn: Well, then, what is?

Grey: I mean, I'm here now and will help, Evelyn. Let's find the truth.

Evelyn: The truth?

Grey: Yes, the truth. The truth about your father's death. The truth about his business. The truth about his sister.

Evelyn: Why? Why do you want to help me?

Grey: Because… because I care about you, Evelyn.Evelyn: You care about me?

Grey: Yes, Evelyn. I care about you. More than you know.

Evelyn: (She looks into his eyes and sees sincerity and warmth.

She feels a surge of emotion and confusion. She doesn't know what to say.) Grey…

Grey: Evelyn, trust me. Please. Let me help you.

Evelyn: (She hesitates for a moment, then nods.) Okay, Grey.

Grey: Thank you, Evelyn. Thank you for trusting me.

Evelyn: Grey. Don't thank me until we find the killer.

Grey: We will, Evelyn. We will find the killer. Together.

Suddenly there was more noise and others were rushing along the passage way to the stateroom. Evelyn and Grey turn back to not miss what is going on.

Sheldon and McClearn edged toward the door leading to starboard. Sheldon had his hands on the knob, when the door opened,and a girl with ash-blond hair, and prominent eyeglasses, burst unceremoniously into the lounge.

A young woman had unsteadily caught hold of the door frame and then walked into the lounge and straight toward the body, "He's dead!" she gasped, as the wide, staring eyes became closely visible to her. "Oh!" she groaned, and sank suddenly to the floor, beside Beckmann. A convulsion of wild sobs shook her body.

The stateroom in a moment is filled with curious concerned guests who all now could be suspects in this tragedy.

"I insist on knowing where I am!" the newcomer announced,

sputteringly, and seized Sheldon by his shirt sleeve. "Can you speak English?"

The girl. Sheldon noted, wore a dark, tailored business suit and a small hat. She looked somehow out of place on a yacht. So did he. for that matter, in his dress shirt and black trousers. McClearn had on an overcoat and a gray felt hat. All three of them locked incongruous. And Sidney Beckmann lying dead in the lounge and the woman with the white hair who had called to him and sobbed over his body!

Who was she anyway? Sheldon understood who Beckmann's child was and had seen her grief. The situation was rapidly becoming mere baffling. And now this girl who babbled on about people not speaking English. Sheldon took her firmly by the arm. and led her down the deck. McClearn followed. The scene in the lounge Sheldon felt, was not the place for this girl. She looked frightened, and quite capable of hysteria

"Who are you?" she demanded. "And why did you two men kidnap me? "

"Please lower your voice." Sheldon cautioned. "We didn't kidnap you. At least, I didn't."

She jerked her arm away. and glared at McClearn. "You did it then."

"I never saw you before in my life," McClearn asserted, gruffly.

"Suppose you tell us who you are and what you are doing on board this yacht?" Sheldon parried, in an effort to calm her.

"Is this a yacht?" she asked, appraisingly.

"Who brought you here?"McClearn questioned.

I don't know. The last thing I remember was that I was standing on the corner outside a club on a Bund street, waiting for a streetcar. It was a little after 10 in the evening. I'd had to stay late, at the office. I saw the car coming and stepped into the street, and something hit me. It may have been a truck that was making a turn behind me. Anyway, I woke up on this boat lying on a bed in quite a nice room. It was daylight. I got up and walked around. I found my way downstairs, and there was a crewman standing in a doorway. He looked like a chef. I asked him a couple of questions, and he began to jibber at me in Chinese, or something. I went back upstairs, and I bumped into a white man in uniform. He looked like an American. I asked him questions, and all he did was jibber like a heathen and make signs."

She halted a moment, and looked from one to the other, and seemed to take on a more aggressive attitude. "Now, look here! If you two didn't kidnap me, for heaven's sake, who did? And why? And for the love of Saint Peter, have these jabbering ninnies put me back into a civilized world. Old man Beckmann would slay me, if my work is not up-to-date, by the time he gets around to the office."

"Who did you say?" McClearn cried.

"Beckmann. Sidney Beckmann, the businessman. I'm secretary in his uptown office. What about it? I have to be at work today,"she snapped, peevishly.

"What's your name?" McClearn pursued. "

My name is Christine Devone.

“Why don't you tell me your names?"

"I'm Dick McClearn, sergeant U.S.Army. And this is Mr. James L. Sheldon – Army officer attached to the Polo team. Am I right?" He turned to Sheldon for confirmation. Sheldon nodded.

"But how - but what" Christine Devone stuttered in confusion."I can't tell you how you or Sheldon came to be aboard, but I was shanghaied,"

McClearn said. "I was having a nice quiet drink, after a hard day at the office. I swear it was my first. The darned thing must have been doped. I woke up on board this yacht. I was in bed and still wearing my overcoat. When I got to strolling around, I met a couple of the crew who jabbered. I went up on the bridge and found a Captain, I guess it was. He jabbered, too. Then I discovered Sheldon."

Sheldon started in with his story, beginning at the point of his first tour of the deck. It was just as he was telling of his experience with the men atop the forecastle, when the sound of running feet caught their attention.

"I say" yelled a voice, "I say you folks just got to talk English" the runner was a slim, under-sized youth, whose oversized cap hung slantingly over one ear. "I say," he panted, breathlessly, as he came abreast of them. "No foohn' you guys gotta" put me ashore. I gotta' get out to the race track this morning. Rangoon’s being shipped South, today. The boss expects me there "

"Bet you are Sidney Beckmann's jockey Stevie West?" McClearn interposed. "Looks like some wise guy had gathered a bunch of Beckmann's employees together for some sinister purpose."

"Sure, I'm West " the little fellow declared hotly, ignoring McClearn's last sentence. "What ya wants' take me off on this schooner for?" –

"Did I ever see you before?" McClearn challenged. "I dunno! You know me. You musta taken me fer a ride when I fell asleep in that their taxi.

"Well we didn't take you for a damn ride," McClearn growled irritably. "We're all in the same boat, and I don't mean maybe. What do you say, Sheldon? Hadn't you better tell Miss Devone and West what happened to Mr. Beckmann?" Both the girl and the jockey looked in astonishment at the suggestion that anything could happen to Mr. Beckmann.

Sheldon related the story, beginning with the moans that he had heard while on deck, and his listeners became wild eyed with consternation. "And it looks." he concluded, "as though we are in for serious trouble. There may be others of Mr. Beckmann employees on board also shanghaied. In fact, I saw a man go into Room I. He'd been seasick. Might as well round him up and find out who he is and what he knows "Funny Business.

"One of us should go back to that woman, McClearn interrupted, thoughtfully. "She may have fainted, or something. Didn't she say, Sheldon, and this was her yacht?" Sheldon nodded grimly. "Funny business! Mighty Funny! I wonder who she is? And if Mr. Beckmann was really related to her?"-

"Where was this other guy?" the jockey put in, quizzically. Sheldon led the way to Room I and knocked on the door.

They waited a moment in silence. Then McClearn knocked, and West rattled the knob noisily.' "Maybe he's dead, too,"

Christine uttered breathlessly. "No use banging down the door until we look around. I'm more curious about that woman we left in the lounge."

Sheldon began to worry about the man in Room I. He might be dead at that, he considered.Might have been poisoned by the same person who killed Beckmann.

He hadn't been dressed like McClearn, West and Miss Devone. He was in pajamas. Beckmann was wearing a nightshirt.

There was some significance in the fact that these two were dressed in sleeping garments, as though prepared for a cruise an indication, perhaps, that neither Beckmann nor the stranger had been shanghaied. For some reason, they might both have been poisoned. He was certain that someone had poisoned Sidney Beckmann. The old man had cried "murder" in his last gasp. The man on the bridge who looked like an American and talked gibberish might be the murderer. For that matter.

Chapter 8

The door of the lounge was hooked open. Voices were clearly audible as the four approached. A man's voice was predominant. Sheldon entered first, and recognized the stout man of Room I whom he had visualized just now as dead. The man was dressed in a dark gray business suit. He looked alert, well-groomed. He was talking conversing with the woman with the white hair. She was standing with her back toward the dead man. The man was facing the doorway, and as he caught sight of the four, he said: "I thought you said that there were two strange men on board? This looks like three, and a woman"

"I am one of Mr. Beckmann's secretaries, Christine Devone began in a shrill voice, which she intended to sound calm, and averted her eyes from the figure on the floor.

"What are you people doing on board Mrs. Cartier – Jason's yacht?" the man barked brusquely.

"Oh! So, this Is Mrs. Cartier-Jason!" Christine said, ironically, and Sheldon, watching her, thought that her eyes betrayed a cynical expression, as though she knew something disagreeable about the lady in the cerise robe.

"I am Mrs. Jason," the woman maintained haughtily. "Mr. Dodge is my lawyer. Will you please, all of you, explain immediately the meaning of your intrusion on my yacht?"

"I was taken for a ride lady honest" West blurted, earnestly, removing his cap, and putting it on over his other ear, with a gesture of nervousness.

"My brother has been murdered," she announced, grimly.

Sheldon wondered why she called herself Mrs. Cartier-Jason, if she had been the one of the Beckmann's family? Strange, also, he thought, that Sidney Beckmann had never mentioned her. And a passing idea gripped his mind that the woman might know something about poisons.

Grey had kept Evelyn away for the center of all this. It was a time to observe and listen… it had become pure confusion with everyone becoming a suspect of sorts.

Now there was a more drama in the lounge – which might have been well-planned. Her surprise at finding strangers on board was well feigned . . .

Mrs. Jason was saying: "All of you will be held on suspicion. There is something very mysterious and funny going on here. Several people smuggled themselves on board my yacht and now a Beckmann murdered"

"Just a moment, Mrs. Jason. Better let me handle the situation," Dodge intervened, suavely. "First, I should like to know" - But whatever he wanted to know was evaded for the moment.

A screech, which was ear-splitting, and seemed to shatter the air, caused all of them to stand petrified for a moment. Another wild howl, and a series of jumbled noises, forced them into action. Dodge darted toward the door at the port side. Others crowded each other in their haste to keep up with him and were met in the doorway by a gesticulating, brown-skinned man, who in his panic, crashed into them, and fell on his knees, frothing at the mouth, muttering Inarticulately, a hideous expression contorting his features.

Dodge seized him by both arms, and jerked him to his feet, Dodge began to talk in the language that sounded like the lingo used by the men on the forecastle, and the white man on the bridge,

Sheldon thought, Ahh…

He seemed - to speak fluently. It was obvious that the brown-skinned man understood, but whatever had terrorized him had bereft him of the power of coherent speech. Dodge shook him. and thundered phrases that sounded like threats.

Mrs. Cartier-Jason kept saying, impatiently: "What's the matter with the darn fool?"

Finally, Dodge dismissed the man, after he had managed a few words. And, mopping his forehead, and with a gesture of nervousness, he said: "This is terrible! The Captain is dead! That native was so frightened, he couldn't talk. From what I could make out he found the Captain on the bridge suffering with pains in his stomach, and ran to get the mate. When he returned, the Captain was dead. These Asians'' always scream and carry on at the sight of death. I suppose the Captain was killed by the same hand that killed Mr. Beckmann. ' It was very unfortunate that I became so beastly seasick the moment we left port. Otherwise, I might have seen something of what was going on around here." "

What are we going to do?" Mrs. Jason asked, frantically. "We all be murdered the next thing we know. These people ought to be put in irons." "I'm thinking about how we are going to make port with only the mate to navigate," Dodge said, huskily.

"Hell!' enunciated Mrs. Jason crossly. "I can run this boat. Why do you think I bought it? I will do my turn on the bridge if that dumb mate can't Stay awake long enough. We cannot be so extremely far out. We did not sail until after midnight, did we? Hurry up and decide what you are going to do with these stowaways, Philip."

Sheldon grinned at the word, remembering the carefully packed suitcase, with his name printed on the tag. He was also conscious of a dual personality displayed by this woman. One moment she possessed distinctly feminine qualities, and in the next to assume an air of masculinity.

McClearn was saying: "We are not stowaways. We were shanghaied, all of us, and put on board while drugged, or something. Whoever is responsible, did not do any slouch job either. I found a suitcase in the closet of that room that I was thrown into, with a tag on it with my name. And the suitcase was filled with brand new clothes that fit me to a T. Some of them even had my initials. I am asking you if we are stowaways or what kind of a put-up job this is anyway?"

"Oh! I didn't know there were closets in the rooms." Christine murmured. "I wonder" " -Cripes!" exclaimed the jockey. "Did you say there was clothes in the closets?" And started toward the door. McClearn halted him.

Mrs. Jason said: "I can't imagine what they are talking about, but I wish you would get busy Philip, and lock these roughnecks up, before they get a chance to kill anyone else. You will have to do something about investigating them, before we get to port and turn them over to the police. The police will think we are only plain stupid, if we don't know something about how they got on here."

"Yes, yes," Dodge replied nervously.

"And I have to go up to the bridge, an verify' this story about the Captain." - - --. "You must place poor Sidney's body in his room, until we get to port. I cannot bear to have him left like this" she paused, and wiped tears from her eyes.; -' –

Sheldon said, politely: "If we can be of any assistance "

"You mind your own " business, young man." she interrupted tartly, and trailed majestically from the lounge." "I shall have to lock all of you in different staterooms,"

Philip Dodge said, sternly. "I shall question you separately."

"You will lock us up in a pig's eye," McClearn sneered belligerently. "There's three of us to one, not counting Miss Devone."

Dodge raised his eyebrows, and clapped his hands.

McClearn made a dash for him, and landed a smashing right fist straight on the jaw. Dodge staggered back, rubbing his jaw. The blow had disconcerted him, but he made no effort to strike back.

McClearn faced him glaringly hands doubled expectantly. The little jockey closed in ready; and Sheldon advanced to one side. Christine picked up a heavy glass tray, and held it aloft.

"You won't gain a thing with your rough stuff.". Dodge said, sourly. The expression in his eyes, made the others turn, four brown-skinned huskies stood in the doorway, eyeing the-scene with bewilderment.

Christine let the ash tray fly.' The heavy glass hit one of them on the chest, and instantly, there was bedlam. Dodge gave frantic orders in the strange lingo. The men sensed a fight, whether or not the orders were heard. McClearn threw off his overcoat, and punched recklessly. " Sheldon tripped one of the men, and sent him sprawling.

West hit wherever he could squeeze in, and Christine Devone unhooked a chair from the floor, and battered one man over the head from behind. He fell forward. Dodge sprang into the fray, and seized the jockey and pummeled him.

McClearn went to Wests aid, with an oath – You miserable coward! he hissed at Dodge.

Chapter 9

The man who West had been attacking lunged forward suddenly, in an effort to tackle Sheldon. and as the latter side-stepped, the man stumbled and fell over the corpse of Sidney Beckmann. He let out a wild shriek gained his feet, and fled screeching from the room. The two on the floor seeing the body writhed and screamed. The man McClearn had exhausted with his wild punches, staggered through the portside door, and fled, squealing at the top of his lungs. McClearn seized one after the other of the two men on the floor, and dragged them onto the deck. He returned triumphantly, and shouted at Dodge. "Who's boss here now?"

“I am, “said a voice from the doorway ' and Mrs. Jason strode angrily into the lounge. She was wearing knickers, and a man's shirt with the sleeves rolled up, and the collar open at the neck.

"You big lummox, you!" she snarled at Dodge. "Don't you know any better than to call those natives in here? You had a sample of how scared they are at the sight or death when that other one came in here yelping. I have had enough yelling and screaming for one morning. I will take charge here. Humph!

You call yourself a lawyer I call you a . . ." She ripped out an unprintable oath, and turned her back on him.

"Well stop the fighting right now," she bawled at the others. Dodge mopped his forehead, cringed slightly, and sat down on a divan, breathing heavily. Mrs. Jason faced Sheldon. with her hands on her hips. "What's your name?" she demanded. He told her, and gave the names of the others.

Sheldon! McClearn! She repeated, frowning. "It seems to me; I've heard those names before."

Sheldon explained their positions with the Beckmann business. McClearn added: "There was several meetings discussing horses with Mr. Beckmann at the track."

'I don't understand this." Mrs. Jason shook her head in bewilderment. "I don't understand this. You all knew or worked for the Beckmann's. You appear uninvited on my yacht and brother and the Captain have been murdered. I need a cup of strong black coffee."

Dodge stood up with alacrity. "I'll get it for you, at once." –

You'll do no such thing!" she exclaimed angrily. "I guess we can all have coffee in the dining room. But before you get any, you go up on that bridge, and attend to the captain's body. And you, Mr. Sheldon, and Mr. McClearn, see if you can carry Sidney's body down to Room B. It's on the port side."

"Do we get breakfast?" the little jockey asked, plaintively.

"Shut up, and help me straighten up this place," she snapped.

Two slightly battered members of the crew served breakfast, in the room adjoining the lounge. There was extraordinarily little conversation. Mrs. Jason had said when she sat down at the table that she had no intention of having her coffee spoiled by any gruesome stories, or anything remotely touching on the two murders.

But it was not a period of relaxation. Every one of them wore a tense expression, as though their suppressed emotions would, at any moment, give way to an explosion. Or some new tragedy would fling itself in their path. When they had finished the meal, Mrs. Jason ordered them to return to the lounge.

"In my opinion, these people should all be locked up, and questioned separately," Dodge objected. "I didn't ask for your opinion,"

Mrs. Jason said, crossly. "I want to hear what these people have to say. I will draw my own conclusions, and make my own plans. Mr. Sheldon, I want you to begin by telling me just how you happened to be on this yacht."

Sheldon told his story, without interruption, and while the others, in turn, told theirs, he watched Mrs. Jason. Her eyes were clear, penetrating, and she stared directly at the person talking. The expression seemed to be one of intense bewilderment. His opinion of her altered considerably. Whoever had kidnaped them, had kept it a secret on the yacht. he was certain. He was also certain that the person responsible for the shanghai trick was also involved in the two murders. And whoever it was, knew the yacht; knew Mr. Beckmann and his business activities, even to the extent of knowing the movements of his employees, and what size clothes they wore.

He looked at the lawyer, and wondered if he had anything to gain by murdering Beckmann, and throwing suspicion on four people who had worked for him. and for some intuitive reason, decided that he had not. The man was obviously afraid of Mrs. Cartier- Jason, and completely under control. Also, the man had undoubtedly been seasick. He looked, even now. as though the yacht's vibration made him uncomfortable. And he appeared to regard the Shanghai stories with genuine amazement.

Sheldon wondered if there were other people on board. He thought or the mate, whom he had not seen, and the engineer was a white man. And made a mental note to look up these two as soon as he was released from the lounge. Then suddenly all eyes were directed toward the starboard doorway, and a voice that had said "May I come in?"

The voice belonged to a stoutish young man, slightly bald, with convex glasses and shifty eyes. He was wearing a dark suit and his shirt was open at the neck. Sheldon stared relentlessly at him, decided that there was a crafty expression about the man's mouth that he did not like. Wondered if he was a Shanghai victim or the master mind behind the situation.

"Come in," Mrs. Jason bellowed. "It's about time you pulled yourself out of bed. All kinds of frightful things have happened. My brother has been murdered, and Captain Mason.

Do we think they were poisoned " "Poisoned? Murdered?" His expression registered unbelief, and changed quickly to one of curious intent, as he asked, "Who are these people?"

"Uninvited guests, who seem to have been forced upon us," Mrs. Jason explained, and turned to the four. "This is my son, Allen Cartier."

Allen Cartier whistled through his teeth, stared blankly at the quartet, and selected a chair, before he drawled, "Which one committed the murders?"

His manner, Sheldon felt, was altogether too nonchalant, and he was puzzled as to the name Cartier, without the Jason.

"We don't know who did anything yet." Mrs. Jason snapped. "The crew sure did plenty of screaming and yelling this morning when I was trying to sleep. Was that when it happened?"

"It seemed rather odd to me that you didn't get up and see what was going on when you heard that racket," Dodge said with a note of scorn.

"They're always yelling for something or nothing," Allen returned carelessly, and then sat forward in his chair as though more vital details were to be discussed.

"I suppose you will have to head into Hawaii now. There will have to be an inquest, and these interlopers will have to be taken to jail. It is an awful nuisance, and it interferes with our project. Somebody will have to relieve that cock-eyed mate on the bridge, too. He was up most of the night."

"I'll do a turn on the bridge," Mrs. Jason announced, "and so can you if necessary."

"I think the mate should be questioned," Sheldon put in.

"I have already questioned him," Dodge said loftily.

"And I have been listening to the stories these folks have to tell." Mrs. Jason said, "and I am not sure that I rang-they had time or inclination to poison anyone "

"So, help me lady!" the little jockey looked owlish.

"What's the plan, then?" Allen inquired.

"They claim to be outfitted with clothes suitable for the cruise. I would like to see some of those clothes." she suggested. "Go put some of 'em on, and in the meantime 1 will go up on the bridge and have a look around." She stood up and looked at Dodge. "Did you tell that dumb ox up there to make for Hawaii?"

Dodge colored slightly. "I'm sorry. In the excitement of getting the captain's body to his quarters, and questioning the mate and some of the crew, I neglected to give explicit orders."

"And you call yourself a lawyer?" she said scathingly. "You come on up there with me now and give that heathen orders. I never did approve of having this Māori tribe on here. When I want to talk, I want to talk English." She stamped out of the room and Dodge followed her.

"Well!" Allen breathed, as they disappeared "It looks like I'm in charge "

“The devil it does," McClearn Interrupted, and stood up with a menacing look in his eyes.

Sheldon intervened quickly. "It's a Funny story, Cartier how four of us who seemed to be in the employ of Mr. Beckmann happened to be abducted and shanghaied on board your mother's yacht. Would you care to hear the details?"

Allen lighted a cigarette and nodded casually. Sheldon related the various incidents concerning all four, and ended with a detailed account of the circumstances under which he had found Sidney Beckmann.

Allen was listening, yet his eyes never once met Sheldon's, nor did he lose his attitude of indifference. He merely grunted once or twice. When Sheldon had finished, Allen remarked: "Circumstantial evidence points to you Sheldon. I wonder why

McClearn did not think of that when he came upon you. Or your story does not click, and was he your accomplice? You may pull the wool over mother's eyes, but you cannot over mine. That tale of all of you being knocked cold and carried on board senseless is too thin. It is also incredible, if you actually had business with the old man before, that none of you had met before. Incidentally, I worked for him myself "

McClearn interrupted hotly: "Did I ever see you before?"

"I don't know. I have no recollection of ever having seen you," Allen returned disagreeably.

"Well, then! Don't you know as well as I do that all of the old man's interests were kept separate, and an employee of one firm never saw those who worked on any of the others, unless there was some special program that concerned the whole outfit? And as for your, big boy, if you are Mrs. Jason's son, and your uncle was the old lady's brother, what are you doing with the name Cartier, and what is she doing with Jason tacked on?"

Allen got to his feet, disregarding McClearn for the moment. His eyes were focused on one of the port side windows, as though something on the far horizon interested him more than the belligerent McClearn.

"Mother was married three times," he said, coldly, "if it interests you to know. The old man disapproved of her first." He left the lounge, and the others saw him go to the port rail, and stand with hands shading his eyes.

There was a moment or two of silence among the four in the lounge. They were waiting for Allen to return.

Then, Christine said: "Well! Of all the mix-ups, this is the worst ever! What are we going to do now? Stand here, looking at each other?"

"Mrs. Jason suggested that she would like to see some of the clothes " Christine continued: “If I have a mysterious suitcase in my closet, it's going to need a lot of explaining, before I wear any of the clothes."

"Gee!" West exclaimed, brightly. "We can all get dressed up! Gosh. I hope they put me in a yachting suit.

Chapter 10

At half past 1 o'clock, a brown-skinned man, clad in a blue uniform, beat a rhythmic tattoo on a huge, brass gong, and luncheon was served. The four shanghaied guests appeared nattily dressed in new clothes. Evelyn and Ebbhart sat together and wanted to be alone.

Mrs. Jason, still wearing knickers and shirt, cast a cynical eye over the group, and glowered speculatively, at the clothes. But she made no remarks.

Allen led off the conversation by asking: "What time do we get to Hawaii, mother?"

"I don't know. Darned if I do not think that that dumb mate has lost the sextant. I cannot find it, any place," she grumbled.

"That shouldn't make any difference," Dodge argued. "You must realize that we must get into Hawaii as soon as possible, on account of the two corpses we are carrying I warned you that you should now be able to communicate with the police. As it is. you are liable to get into serious difficulties if we don't make Hawaii as soon as possible."

"Then go up and wrangle with that heathenish mate," she snarled. "Make him find the sextant." A long, uncomfortable silence followed, and as the coffee was served.

Allen said: "By the way. where are you keeping the bodies?

We took the Captain's body to his quarters. Your mother ordered Mr. Sheldon and Mr. McClearn to place Mr. Beckmann's body in Room B," Dodge replied, stiffly. 'But I looked in' the Captain's quarters, and I looked in Room B, and they are both empty," Allen declared. '

Mrs. Jason stood up. excitement blazing in her eyes. "What's that? What did you say?"

"I said that Capt. Mason's body is not in his quarters, and neither is Uncle Beckmann's body in his room.' Allen said, distinctly.

"Did you look in Room B?" Sheldon asked, concernedly. Allen nodded, and reached to another piece of cake

. "We must see about this," blustered Dodge, and strode rapidly from the room. The others followed. Allen straggling in the rear, munching on the cake.

They went directly to Room B. Dodge opened the door. The room held an atmosphere of quiet peace, with its window curtains drawn. But there was no one there.

Mrs. Jason began to weep.

"We laid the body on this bed," Sheldon stammered, in great perplexity.

"Maybe you went into the wrong room, by mistake?" Christine suggested.

Dodge stepped back on deck, and flung open the door of Room C. They stared all of them into another empty room.

"Room A." he announced, tersely, "is Mrs. Jason' quarters. She has had occasion to go in there within the last hour or two, so there is no need of looking in there." He turned menacingly to Sheldon and McClearn, and demanded, "Where did you put Mr. Beckmann's body?"

"Did you hear Cartier say that the Captain's body is not where you are supposed to have left it?" McClearn asked, sharply.

Dodge ignored him. He was talking to Mrs. Jason. "I warned you about these two men. Their actions have been suspicious from the first. You will agree now that you should have allowed me to lock them up when I wanted to. This thing would not have occurred if I had been in charge."

"No use going off the deep end. yet," Allen interfered. "The bodies must be about, somewhere. Nobody would have taken a chance on throwing them overboard in broad daylight, with all of us around Let's organize a search."

"We'll organize a search, all right " Dodge declared, firmly. "But first of all, these two men are going to be locked up, before anything else happens."

"I intend to see if the Captain's body is where you were supposed to have put it " McClearn asserted, stubbornly.

"You'll see the inside of a jail before long," Dodge growled, and seized McClearn from behind, pinning both arms back so quickly that McClearn was caught unawares. "Come on, Allen, grab Sheldon Well have no more nonsense."

Sheldon made a quick lunge toward Dodge, but Allen sprang forward and overpowered him. West closed in with a few wild punches, aimed at Allen, and Christine Devone clawed malevolently at Dodge, scratching his wrists.

"You little hell-cat!" Mrs. Jason yelled, forgetting her tears. She caught hold the girl's sleeve and shook her roughly.

Christine scratched at her, but the older woman managed to get hold of both wrists and dragged her forcibly down the deck.

In the midst of this scuffle, one of the crew emerged from the region of the quarterdeck and stood gaping. Dodge rasped out an order and immediately two other brown-skinned men came leaping into the fray. Dodge released McClearn in the clutches of the first man. The other two attacked Sheldon and West. Mrs. Jason continued to propel Christine down the deck, struggling.

In less than three minutes the four were locked up in separate staterooms. Sheldon, bruised and disheveled, found himself in a strange room. He heard Dodge's voice with a staccato inflection, babbling the strange words of the lingo used by the crew, for a moment or two, heard the men walking away, and then everything was quiet. His head throbbed miserably. In the excitement of swiftly moving events, he had forgotten the headache. He stretched out on the bed. wearily, and his eyes strayed absently over the room.

A man's shirt was tossed over one chair, a pair of trousers over another. Two pairs of shoes had been pushed under the dressing-table. Brushes and other accessories were scattered about. And suddenly Sheldon sat up, alert. This room had been occupied by one of the men. Which man? The clothing indicated that the man was large. Therefore, it was neither McClearn nor West. But it might be that either Cartier or Dodge had occupied the room. He sprang into action, intent upon examining the contents of the room before anyone discovered that he had been put there in error. And began by ransacking the desk.

A few blank sheets of paper and envelopes filled the cubbyholes, and under these, in one of the recesses he came upon a letter address to Allen Cartier 12 Vineland Street. Brooklyn. N. Y. He fumbled with the envelope and drew out a folded sheet of paper, and grinned, thinking what a good opportunity this to do a little detective work pin- on Allen.

The sheet of paper was filled with closely lettered writing that looked like a woman. He turned the sheet over, for the signature, and discovered the word "Christine." Flipped it over again and read: "Darling:

I am afraid that something drastic will have to be done before your Uncle approves of our engagement. He said yesterday, in the office, that he was violently opposed to a marriage between us. He said almost resigned. But on account of you know what I managed to control my temper. We must think of something, and think of it quickly, otherwise we will both be miserable."

Sheldon paused, and turned to the signature again. "Christine." he reflected, might easily be Christine Devone. For all he knew, she might have been lying about waiting for a streetcar at 10 o'clock at night. He seemed to remember that she had been bewildered and nervous when he had first seen her. But then, she had told what sounded like a straight story, and she had told it before either he or McClearn had offered theirs. She might be a consummate little actress. She might be involved with Allen in the "something drastic." And that something might have resulted in murder. His hand trembled slightly as he held the letter and tried to think of intricate plans that must have been made, in order to have created the present situation. But. I of course, there were other Christine's in the world. In fact, the name was common ...

Footsteps sounded on the deck. and he crumpled the letter and shoved it into his pocket and sat back on the bed.

Someone walked past the door and kept on. He returned to the desk and pulled open the top drawer. Several stiff sheets of paper, folded and held together by an elastic band, covered a small, leather folder that contained newspaper clippings. He loosened the stiff papers and noted that they had the appearance of a legal document.

Other footsteps along the deck were audible. Someone stopped outside the room door. He had just time to conceal the papers in an inside pocket of his coat and drop back on the bed before a key grated in the lock and the door opened.

Chapter 11

Allen Cartier stood framed in the doorway. A look of extreme annoyance governed his features. "Of all the nerve!" he exclaimed, angrily. "What are you doing in my room?”

Sheldon answered: "I was pushed in here, and locked in. What about it?" "

Humph! Another mistake of Philip's I suppose. Do you remember the letter of the room that you were in before?"

"Listen, Cartier," Sheldon said crossly, ignoring the question. "What do you hope to gain by this tough stuff locking us up? On the face of it, does it seem possible that either McClearn or I killed Sidney Beckmann? And as for the Captain, what motive could we have had for killing him?"

There was a crafty look in Allen's eyes, as he drawled. "Well, I don't know you. I do not know that you were ever betting horses with the old man. I know that there was a chap by the name of James L. Sheldon that was exceedingly popular around the track and polo field. How am I to know that you are not posing under that name? That story of you being put on board, unconscious, looks fishy to me. My guess is, that the four of you had some purpose in coming aboard, so you sneaked on. and made up a dramatic story.

Of course, your purpose was to get rid of the old man. I do not know what you expected to gain by it. But one would suppose it was something. If just one of you had been on board, I guess you thought you would not have stood a chance at not being caught, however with the four of you cooking up a fancy story, it looked easy. As for the Captain, he probably got suspicious, and you bumped him off for knowing too much." He slumped into a convenient chair, and lighted a cigarette. If the Captain could not speak English, he could not have heard much to be suspicious about,"

Sheldon objected.

"You don't know this Māori outfit. They are a suspicious lot, and I did not say that he had heard anything. He may have seen something."

"Did you find the bodies?" Sheldon asked, after a pause, in which he considered many angles.

"No," Allen muttered sullenly. "Come on, which room were you in before? I don't want to have you squatting on my bunk all day." He reached over to the wall and pressed a button.

Sheldon: "You think that my story and McClearn's was cooked up. What about West's story, and Christine's?" He mentioned the girls name with particular emphasis, and looked hard at Allen.

Allen blinked, and shifted uneasily. "Aw! Shut up! I am in no mood to talk about it. All my plans have been upset " There was a discreet knock at the door, and Allen admitted one of the Māori's. He said a few words in the unknown language, haltingly some to made motions.

It was evident to Sheldon that he was not as well acquainted with the lingo as Dodge. The man looked a little uncertain, and

Sheldon said, fiercely: Look here, Cartier, if you are thinking of having this sailor manhandle me again. I'll never rest until I give you a good licking. I'll go to Room F by myself, and you can lock me up, if you are tired of my company. But send that crewman away."

Allen waved the man away with a careless gesture, and lit another cigarette. Sheldon edged toward the door before Allen stood up. He thought vaguely of making a get- away, but realized that it was useless and, besides, he was anxious to examine the documents he had taken, and the clippings. Cabin "F" proved to be next to Allen's room. Sheldon walked in there and Allen pushed him inside and thrust the key in the lock and clicked it quickly.

As soon as his footsteps died away, Sheldon recovered the papers from his suit pocket. He spread out the legal document and saw at once it was presumably a copy of Sidney Beckmann's last will and testament. He scanned it briefly, and learned that Philip Dodge was named as one of the executors. Five million dollars was divided in equal shares. To his beloved sister Mathilda Beckmann Cartier-Jason," his "faithful workers, McClearn, Christine Davone and to "the best jockey in America, Stevie West."

Sheldon whistled softly. It came as a complete surprise that Sidney Beckmann had planned to leave any such magnificent amount to anyone. There was a deep significance, also, in the fact that the other three, who were to receive an equal share were participants of this mysterious voyage. Allen's Name Omitted. There were other small bequests, to servants and friends. Sheldon read the list carefully. Noted that Allen Cartier's name was not included. Went over the list again. The name was not there. He wondered what Allen had done to displease the old man. And thought of the letter signed "Christine."

He removed the clippings from the leather folder, and scanned the top one. It was too dark to read newspaper print, comfortably. Stood up to reach the light switch, and wondered suddenly if they were within sight of land? Looked out of the window, half expecting to see tiny flecks of light glowing in the distance was disappointed. Remembered that this room faced starboard side and snapped on the light.

He read first clear clipping, a short piece, that Mr. and Mrs. Charles Devone announced, the engagement of their daughter, Christine, to Mr. Allen Cartier and was not surprised. He was certain now, that Allen was the murderer. Thought that Allen had conceived the weird plan of snatching McClearn and himself in order to establish a semblance of guilt. Christine Davone's story was entirely untrue, and had been part of the plan. And for some indefinable reason, he entertained doubts concerning West. Perhaps, because Allen had seemed as disinterested at the mention of the jockey's name, as at the girls. There was also, the fact, that both the girl and West, had claimed not to have investigated the room closets, until after McClearn had mentioned finding the suitcase in his.

Probably, he reasoned, Sidney Beckmann had been bitter about Christine's engagement to Allen. Probably the drastic thing that Allen had decided upon was murder. The million dollars that Christine would inherit was motive enough. Beckmann may have threatened to cut her off. And Allen, in his haste to forestall this measure, must have schemed accordingly. The date on the clipping was scarcely a month old.

The situation was narrowing down. It had been planned that he should discover Sidney Beckmann, dying, and that McClearn should be in the lounge when Mrs. Jason entered. He could not figure exactly how this plan had been arranged, but on the face of it there was a feasible idea, and quite enough to convince a jury of their guilt. Allen had been quick to mention "circumstantial evidence." He couldn't quite fit in the purpose of having West on board. No doubt there was some underlying motive. He began to wonder if Mrs. Jason was as innocent as she had appeared when listening to their stories? Remembered that she had dragged Christine along the deck in a frenzy that was far from gentle, and recalled the cynical expression with which Christine had regarded the older woman, at their first meeting. He decided that Mrs. Jason was being victimized. And Dodge? Allen did not seem to be clever enough to pull off any such nefarious scheme alone.

Dodge, with a lawyer's ability to work out details, might have aided Allen. On the other hand. Allen might have counted on the other's lethargy, as the result of seasickness. The man had been seasick. Some people are always seasick on the water. Dodge might be one of those people, and Allen had known it. He had had Christine to connive with. She looked smart enough to plot and engineer an intrigue.

Allen had mentioned some project, which getting to Hawaii would be interfered with. The two corpses had been disposed of. thereby preventing an autopsy that would reveal an analysis of the poison used. The sextant had been hidden to confuse the navigator. The "project." undoubtedly, was premediated crime, and would involve further crime.

He shuddered, dismally, and turned to the next clipping. The article was from a California newspaper with a clear by line. The reporter was a Grey Ebbhart. Ahh... and with a slight smile he remembered Evelyn’s friend and the unsettling dinner at the Astor House. Ebbhart was that uninvite guest looking for another story.

All probably to bring closure to his first mystery. Connections are coming together.

This pertained to the history of the yacht Golden Eagle. A prominent copper magnate had originally owned the Golden Eagle. The name in the opening paragraph was somewhat blurred. It looked like Ontagu. Māori officers and crew had manned the Golden Eagle, and during a world cruise, Mr. James Sheldon drew the clipping closer, and made out the name Cartier, and continued avidly. "Mrs. Alice Beckmann" the clipping stated died suddenly, and was buried in mid- Pacific. The cause of her death is said to be unknown, and there is a certain element of mystery surrounding the meager details given to the press." In a final paragraph it was mentioned that Mr. Beckmann had been divorced in 1922 and that his former wife had subsequently married Stephen Jason, a wealthy Wall Street broker. Beckmann's sister's son, Allen Cartier, had been with an Uncle Jason on the world cruise.

Another clipping, again with a Ebbhart byline, told of the late Anthony Cartier's will. The entire residue of the estate, amounting to three million dollars, had been left to Allen Cartier. Sheldon whistled. If Allen had inherited three million dollars in 1923, which was the date of the clipping why " There were too many "whys" to be considered at the moment. Sheldon fingered the next clipping, eagerly "Millionaire Playboy is Bankrupt," was the caption under date of September 28, 1924. Allen, according to this item, had lost a fortune in Wall Street. The last clipping was dated

May 1925. and recorded the sale of the yacht Golden Eagle, which had been put up at auction for the second time, since 1923, and had been purchased by Mrs. Cartier-Jason, who had at one time been the wife of the original owner.

A key scraped in the lock. Sheldon, started from his contemplations, tossed the clippings and the copy of the will into the drawer of the bedside table, closed it, and tried to look at ease.

The door opened, and Dodge entered, followed by one of the crew, who was bearing a napkin-covered tray.

. "What time do we get into Hawaii?" Sheldon queried, affably.

"Can't say," Dodge returned, shortly. "Are you anxious to spend the night in jail?"

"I don't know why I should spend the night in jail. I can prove that I was shanghaied." He couldn't, of course, but he wanted to see if this statement would have any effect upon Dodge. But the latter only shrugged, indifferently.

Then, in a more friendly tone, he said: "To be frank. I was inclined to believe your story, fantastic as it seemed, until we discovered that Mr. Beckmann's body was missing."

"What about the Captain? you were supposed to have seen that his body was placed in his quarters. Have they found his body?"

"No," Dodge passed a hand through his hair with a weary gesture, and sat down on the foot of the bed. The Māori had placed the tray on the table, uncovered it, and arranged the food. Dodge waved him away. "I have been so cussed seasick." he began, "that I can’t seem to realize the enormity of all that has happened, or what is back of it. Would you mind telling me what your theory is?"

My theory wouldn't hold water, I'm afraid," Sheldon answered, cautiously. "What do you think of McClearn?" I think his story is as true as mine is."

"Vicious temper!" Dodge stated, and shivered, involuntarily. "I've just been talking to him." He sighed, as though the conversation had been distinctly unpleasant, and glanced at his watch. "It's after seven. I told Mrs. Jason that I would join her for dinner at quarter past. Think it over. Sheldon. and if you decide to discuss your theory with me. Before we land, push the button there, and I'll drop around.

Chapter 12

When he had gone, Sheldon looked at the food spread out on the tray He did not feel particularly hungry, and it occurred to him that Mr. Beckmann and the Captain were probably poisoned by something that had been put in food, according to his own theory, there were dubious indications of further crimes. He sniffed at each portion of food. Thought that there was a peculiar odor about the salad, and pushed it aside. The potato had been baked, and the skin unbroken He pried it open, and nibbled at the potato.

A faint tap on the window startled him. He turned, quickly, and drew back in alarm, at the sight of a face pressed closely against the darkly shadowed glass. Sheldon's immediate reaction was that someone was spying upon him. and had inadvertently made a sound on the windowpane. Then, as he stared, the features of the little jockey became clear, and with a sense of relief, he saw that West was motioning him to open the window. He raised It with the least possible sound, and West whispered: "I'm coming In." He scrambled up to the ledge, squeezed through the narrow opening, and dropped into the room. Sheldon eased the window down.

"Lucky, I'm small, West breathed.

"Gee! It was lonesome! I have da' have somebody to talk to so I did a scram outer my window. Say, do you think they are going to pinch us?"

"Sit down," Sheldon said, and the tray happened to catch his attention. "If that crewman comes for this, you'd better duck under the bed.

"You didn't eat much," West observed...

Sheldon: "Wasn't hungry."

"Gee! I was. I cleared the plates, and the steward was right back after my tray."

Sheldon: I am playing Sherlock Holmes. "See here. West. I'm going to ask you a few questions,' he said tentatively.

"By the way McClearn and I were grabbed. It. looks as though we were to be accused of murder ".

"Sure does! the little Jockey's eyes were bulging with suspense. "Whatever you may think, my story of being shanghaied was true. Was yours?" I hope to die this minute if every word wasn't the gospel truth, he proclaimed. earnestly.

Sheldon: "You had known Mr. Beckmann for quite a few years? Is that right? The jockey nodded. "Had he mentioned to you that he planned to make a cruise on this yacht?"

"Nope. Say, you going to' play Sherlock Holmes?"

Sheldon smiled.

West says: "Somebody has to." "And I'm going to be Watson – Ok Sherlock, shoot the works.'

Sheldon: Did anyone ever tell you that Mr. Beckmann had mentioned you in his will?"

"Who. me?" West gulped. In astonishment. "Geez! No. The old boy was always after me not to be too reckless spending' me dough. Said I was living' too wild. Of course, I been wild drinking' and chasing after the skirts. But I promised the old man a month or two ago, that I'd cut it out. So, I went an' took the pledge. I am not even had a mouthful of ginger ale since."

Sheldon laughed softly, and reflected that the date on the copy of the will was fairly recent. "Did you ever see this fellow. Allen Cartier, before?"

"Yeah! I think I seen. him a couple' times at the races with the old girl."

Sheldon: "Did you ever talk with him?"

West: "Mebbe said something' or other about the way the bets was running'.

Sheldon: "But you are not sure?"

West: "It's like this. Mr. Beckmann used to bring people out now and then was thinking' awhile back, that this Allen and his ma was with him sometimes. Most generally, the folks that was with Mr. Beckmann use to' kid me about this horse, Rangoon. 'cause I'm nuts on that horse. Gee! I was supposed to be out at the stables this morning'. Did they cut out racing' in Hawaii?

You know that Rangoon has to be shipped south. What was you saying' about that there will? Did I think he'd left me chunk?" "That's It." "Gee! I could sure use five grand, all right."

Sheldon: "And still keep the pledge?"

West: "Sure. that'd be easy now. My wild oats has all been sunk under six feet." What would you do with a lot of money?" Me? I'd build pop and mum a place in the country, so they could raise chickens, ducks, and things." He eyed Sheldon speculatively, and added: "Who was telling' you the grand news?"

I am not at liberty to say, just now, Sheldon answered, and changed the subject. "Did you come straight here from your room, or did you look in on McClearn?"

Gosh! I forgot to tell you the news! McClearn busted out. My room is right next to his, on the other side of the deck, an awhile before Dodge led the way in with my tray of grub, I heard a lot of banging 'round next door, an' the first thing I knew, I seen McClearn running hastily my window " "Did they catch him?' "I am not sure. Oh, an' say, another thing, after I did a scram out the window, I heard voices in that lounge room, and I ducked down there an' listened under the window.

Allen was in there, telling his mother that McClearn had chucked the bodies overboard, so-is not if a be complicated with, any blame for poison in' 'em." "That's ridiculous! He couldn't have thrown the bodies overboard single-handed. And when did he have an opportunity? The only time we were separated was when we all went to change our clothes. He couldn't have managed it, even with help in broad daylight, without someone seeing him.

Sheldon: “Did Allen give "any details?"

West: "Nope. He kept saying'- that he didn't see how McClearn did it."

"He didn't!" Sheldon scoffed, and after a minute, asked: "Any sight of land over on the port side?"

West: "Oh. gee! I never thought of that. We ought to be getting' in soon, at that. I wonder "

"Hush!" Sheldon warned, "and crawl under the bed." A key clicked as West disappeared under the bed. The Māori who had brought the tray entered. Allen was right behind him.

The latter looked cross and uneasy. "See here, Sheldon," he began, crisply. "You monkeyed in my desk when you were in Room G. You took some papers that belong to me. I want 'em." The Māori picked up the tray and left the room, noiselessly.

Sheldon grinned, slyly. "How many questions are you willing to answer in order to get those papers back?

Allen flushed angrily. "I'm not answering any questions. I'm getting those papers." The doorknob turned with the faintest squeak, and Sheldon jumped to his feet. He suspected that Allen had given the Māori orders to leave the tray somewhere and return. He dreaded another scuffle, and with nerves tensed watched the door open inch by inch.

Dick McClearn ' stepped into the room, and as he slammed the door with one hand the other gripped Allen's coat collar and jerked that surprised young man backward. Then McClearn's left fist shot out and crashed Allen's jaw. He stumbled over a chair and fell in a heap on the floor, his head striking the bed post. McClearn yanked a piece of rope from his pocket and seized Allen's feet. "Hold his hands there, Sheldon," he ordered.

Sheldon with grim amusement obeyed the order. McClearn knotted the rope around the ankles and severed the dangling end with a Docket knife, and made swift work of tying the hands together. Allen whimpered, squirmed, and cursed.

"Want me to sit on his stomach?" a voice squeaked gleefully, and West crawled from under the bed.

So you're here," McClearn said. "You might help Sheldon and me lift him onto a chair. I mean to have a few words with this guy."

McClearn was now planning a mutiny to obtain entrance to Engineer's private quarters and asked that Sheldon do his best to talk matters over with Mrs. Cartier- Jason.

Chapter 13

He jerked Allen roughly by one arm. Sheldon took the other, West caught him about the knees, and altogether they pulled him into a chair.

"What Is the meaning of this? You crooks!" Allen puffed belligerently.

I'll tell you." McClearn' blared. "We are not even in sight of land. We are not even headed for Hawaii. Your mother claims that she lost the sextant end can't get her bearings. If anybody stole the thing you did. And when I let you out of this room you are going up on that bridge, and I'm going to tie you there and torture you until you think of a way of getting to Hawaii.

Allen sneered: "You'd have to fight six husky natives first and there's Dodge and my mother to consider."

Don't I know that you are double-crossing your mother you big bum!" McClearn rapped back.

'Gee!" murmured the little jockey, admiringly. "We got a regular sheriff with us."

Wait a minute." Sheldon interrupted the very irritable McClearn. 'Before we get into an argument. What's your plan?".

"Come into the bathroom, where this swine can't hear us. And you, West, stand guard.

We'll let you in on it later little boy."

West winked. "Okey. Sheriff!"

In the bathroom, with the door closed. McClearn said: "I've been wanting to have a pow-wow with you. When we scattered to get downstairs. I knew Mrs. Jason would get a squint at the mate, off duty. Also wanted to see what the engineer looked like, if any. I didn't have to go far when I heard voices

A couple of men were having a chat, and. unbelievably. they were talking in English, and they sounded as mad as blazes. They were talking at first about the Captain's death. It didn't take me long to discover that they were the very men I was hoping to find. The mate and the engineer. One of them wanted to start on the rampage and mutiny. The other one objected and talked about money and a 'master mind.' I gathered from other scraps of conversation that these two and the Captain had been on this yacht for years, and that it had been owned in 1923 by Allen Cartier's father. They talked mysteriously about his death at sea arid how he had been buried in the Pacific.

There was a "master mind' and money involved about that, then they began laughing aloud Mrs. Jason, and how Allen was trying to nut it over on her by having them pretend that they couldn't speak English. One of them. I think it was the engineer, wanted to go to Mrs. Jason and tell her a few things about her darling son. It seems the poor old girl can't navigate very well, and because she has lost the sextant, she can't get her bearings. She won't trust the mate topside there for more than an hour or two, and just as he gets the yacht 'headed toward land she comes back and flops it about in the other direction.

"They talked about some project on a place called Dawn Island that Allen has up his sleeve. One oi them argued that the Captain was the only one beside the 'master mind' who had known all the details. They cursed about 'extra people' being put on board, and one of them said that the Captain objected to this. I also learned that just before the Golden Eagle put up steam last night the Captain and Allen and Mr. Beckmann had a drink together, and Allen and the old man had an argument."

"Did they say anything about disposing of the bodies?' Sheldon asked.

"No. They wouldn't be apt to have had anything to do with that. I have an idea that whoever disposed of the bodies threw them overboard just about the time that I was down there listening-in. Everyone was supposed to be busy changing their clothes about that time."

Sheldon decided that it would be unwise to mention the fact that anyone suspected him of being the guilty party. He had no wish to excite McClearn's temper to a further pitch.,.

"Later, when I was locked in the stateroom," McClearn was saying, "I had plenty of time to think, and I decided that at the first opportunity I would talk the matter over with you, and if you agree we'll help these two guys start a mutiny. I didn't like the idea of being shut up and not knowing what was going on, so when Dodge came stalking in with his lordly manner, behind the steward with the tray, I socked him one on the nose and ran like the devil. Dodge and the steward caught me, and I was clamped into a room down 'below.

About ten minutes later two of the natives came along with a tray, without Dodge. I shelled out about half the green-backs I had and waved them at the crew and made passes, toward the door. Maybe those natives can't talk English, but they know how to talk to green backs in their own gibberish. I didn't stop to eat, I just sneaked out behind them and up the steps.

The first person I see marching along the deck is our friend Allen, but I take care that he doesn't see me. I thought he might be going to his own room, but when he passed it and came in here, it was just my meat, because I was trying to figure how to get in to talk things over with you. "Well! What do you say to a little high-class mutiny?" "The whole thing is so darned complicated," Sheldon answered thoughtfully. "It's hard to tell who to trust. You didn't get a look at the two men you heard talking, did you?"

"No. What difference does it make? I tell you. Sheldon, you, and I' are up against it. That dog-gone stuffed shirt of a lawyer is going to pin the murder of Sidney Beckmann on us. Allen, the big goof, is going to help him do it. They are going to say that Mrs. Jason went to the lounge in search of her brother, and found us standing over his dead body. No jury in the world is going to believe that we were shanghaied. And how the deuce are we going to prove that we were?

To tell you the truth. Sheldon. old man. I had a funny feeling when I found out that Beckmann was dead, and you there alone with him." "I have thought of that, and so did Allen. Only he doesn't believe you found me there alone. Thinks we killed him together."

"The dumb ox! Whatever kind of poison that was. it took time for a person to die. As soon as I realized that it was poison that the old man had died of. I knew that you had nothing to do with it."

"Thanks." Sheldon responded, and added, "Suppose we go have a little talk with the daughter and her new friend. The pair of them are getting spooky. Evelyn is packing around a sketch pad and friend Ebbhart is making an effort to take notes on everything anyone does.

Mac and Sheldon set off down a passageway and in a short time finds Evelyn with Grey in a small office.

Sheldon: Evelyn, we need to talk. Evelyn: What is it? She looked nervous.

Sheldon: It’s about the investigation. It doesn’t seem some

people are taking it seriously. They're too busy questioning us and searching the yacht. They're not looking for the real killer.

Evelyn: I know, Grey and I agree. But what can we do? We're not detectives. We're not experts.

Sheldon: No, we're not either. But we have something they don't have.

Evelyn: What's that?

Sheldon: We have your Aunt.

Evelyn: My Aunt?

Shelton: Yes, your Aunt. Mrs. Jason. She's a brilliant woman. She was married to a former prosecutor. She knows the law. She knows how to handle a case like this.

Evelyn: She does?

Grey: Of course she does. She's been following the leads. She's been reading reports. She's even given us a break to get involved.

Evelyn: She has?

Sheldon: Yes, she has. And she has some ideas. Some theories.

Evelyn: She does?

Grey: I agree, I believe she wants to help settle this.

Evelyn: She does?

Grey: Yes, she does. Evelyn, listen to them. Your Aunt is our best chance to find the truth. To find justice for your father.

Evelyn: But how? How can she help us?

Sheldon: She can help us by taking charge of the investigation. Mac and I will direct our efforts. On the surface she will provide us advice and guidance.

Evelyn: But how? How can she do that?

Sheldon: This yacht is not that large that we can't find her, and she will be communicating with us through me.

Grey: Yes, Evelyn. Don't you see? It's perfect. No one will suspect anything. No one will know what we're doing.

Evelyn: But what are we doing?

Grey: We're doing our own investigation, Evelyn. We're gathering evidence. We're interviewing witnesses. We're analyzing clues. We're writing everything down. Everything.

Evelyn: Writing everything down?

Grey: Yes, Evelyn. Writing everything down. That's the key. That's the secret. That's how we'll sort out the suspects. That's how we'll find the killer.

Evelyn: (She looks into his eyes and sees determination and confidence. She feels a surge of hope and courage. She nods.) Okay, guys. Okay. I trust you all to make progress before we reach port.

Grey: We will, Evelyn. We will find the killer. Together.

Sheldon nods and suggests: What about the mate and engineer, you think they are down below now?"

Grey: "We can look. What will we do with Allen?"

Sheldon:"Leave him there. I think we can trust West to watch him until we get back. You don't happen to know where Dodge is do you?"

Grey: "I don't. But it's dark, I think we should be able to evade him. Come on."

McClearn returned to the cabin opened the door, and said to West, with a wink. "We be taking a stroll around the deck for exercise. Be back in a few minutes. Hold everything while we are gone.'

"You bet!" the little jockey winked back, and to show his nerve, punches Allen on the jaw.

"Don't be brutal," McClearn cautioned lightly.

"What do you think of West?"'! Sheldon asked when they were well, down the deck.

"Okey. Why? Wasn't he shanghaied the same as we were?'

"I'm wondering." Sheldon pursued. "What do you think of the girl?"

"Don't like her much. Couldn't say why. except that she carries an artificial manner that disagrees, with my digestion. what are you getting at?"

Sheldon:"I don't know. But I don't think her story is on the level."

"Humph!" McClearn grunted. "She told hers first, didn't she?"

Sheldon:"That's right. But I have reason to believe that she lied." "What room is she supposed to be in?" "I think it's J. Right next to the lounge."

"Let's see If she's there." McClearn proposed. They knocked several time on the door of Room J. There was no response 'Well be back," McClearn said ' cynically.' "Maybe" she's dead too." They went through the empty dining-room, and down a short flight of steps to a lower passage.

McClearn led the way, and stopped at a door that was lettered PLEASE KEEP OUT and knocked. A voice from within bellowed a series of incomprehensible syllables. "Listen," McClearn contended. "You can talk English. Mr. Engineer. I heard you talking to the mate. Be a sport and let me in. I'm one of the uninvited guests on this yacht, and I have certain suspicions that agree with yours. We may be able to get together on them.," He waited a few seconds. Heard the man moving about and became impatient.

"Hey! Are you going to let me in?"

"Are you alone?" queried a gruff voice that sounded somehow different in English than in the other language.

"Sure," and McClearn whispered to Sheldon, "Better for me to see him alone. Go back to your room, and I'll see you later."

Sheldon did not go back to his room just then. He wanted time to think over the things that McClearn had told him. Allen and the jockey were in his room, and there would be another argument. He leaned over the rail of the port side, and stared into the turbulent water. The rain had ceased, but the sky was cloudy and cast a gloomy reflection on the water. He wondered who had suggested to Allen that McClearn had thrown the two bodies overboard. And if Mrs. Jason believed it. Decided to go up on the bridge and have a talk with her.

Mrs. Jason was on the bridge, staring straight ahead. As Sheldon opened the door she said: "I wish I could find that darned sextant by. morning, so that I can find out where we are going."

"Can I help you look for it?" Sheldon asked politely. She turned, and her eyes rested uncertainly on Sheldon for half a minute. "If anybody can help anyone in this mess. I'd be grateful." She sighed heavily and continued to scrutinize Sheldon as though measuring his ability. And added: "I am not the best navigator in the world. Never did know where I was going in the dark."

Sheldon: "Couldn't your son relieve you?"

Mrs. Jason: "He could if he weren't too busy thinking, he's a detective. Can't blame him for that. After what happened today. Whoever could have killed my brother Sidney? The poor, old soul didn't have an enemy in the world. Most generous hearted creature that ever lived. And as if it weren't enough to kill him. someone had to go and throw the body overboard."

"Do you know who did that?" Sheldon asked gravely:

Mrs. Jason: "If I did, I'd choke him with my own hands. Allen says that McClearn fellow has been running amuck. He thinks he did it, but I don't know."

"McClearn has a violent temper," Sheldon defended. "He's furious, naturally, at the deal - that's been handed to us. But. even if he had the inclination which I am sure he hadn't it would not have been possible for him to have disposed of the two bodies single-handed. The crew don't speak English, so he could not have ordered any of them to do it."

"That's reasonable. she mused absently, "but Allen is very suspicious of him. He suspects you too. And he doesn't believe those wild stories that you folks told him about being shanghaied."

Sheldon shrugged: These were strange stories. I don't blame anyone for being skeptical. I can hardly believe that what happened to me is true.": The mate is found dead with a tube of powdered flask nearby.

Chapter 14

"Haven't you any idea about who might have put you on board? Were you unconscious all the time?" she asked.

Sheldon: "Yes—l was. The first thing I thought of when I woke up on board here was somebody had mistaken me for someone else. Then I found the suitcase with clothes that seemed to have been made for me. Later, when I came upon Mr. Beckmann, I knew that there was some mysterious purpose behind my being here. May I ask what time you came aboard yesterday."

Mrs. Jason: "It was sometime early in the evening. Allen said that we would: not sail before midnight. So Sidney and I came on a little while after dinner."

Sheldon: "Did you retire before the yacht sailed?"

Mrs. Jason "I did. I was dog tired. I stayed' up as long as I could. I left Sidney reading in the lounge. He said he wasn't tired. I'd been in bed a couple of hours when I heard a commotion, and I trailed up to the lounge to see what it was. I never did find out what it was. Sidney and Allen were in the lounge. They said they hadn't heard anything. We had just left the dock."

Sheldon: "What kind of a drink were they having? Did they have anything to eat with it? And where was Dodge at the time?'

Mrs. Jason:"Say! Who do you think you are? Asking so many fool questions?" She seemed suddenly aware that he had assumed an interrogative attitude and to remember, also, that he was supposed to be confined to his room. "I thought you were locked up. Who let you out?" she demanded explosively.

Sheldon:1 walked out easy enough," he retaliated calmly. "I've been suspected of murder. It's only fair that I should have an opportunity to investigate. Also, I had a very deep personal regard for Mr. Beckmann, and no one is more anxious than I to find the real murderer. I can see no reason I should not ask you a few questions."

His voice held a quality of determination to acknowledge, however reluctant.

"Well!" her tone was flat.

Sheldon: "What were they drinking?" he asked tersely.

Mrs. Jason: "Whiskey sour, I think. If they had anything to eat with it, I didn't see anything," she answered sullenly.

Sheldon: "And Mr. Dodge?"

Mrs. Jason: "He. was in bed. He always gets seasick as soon as he gets on a boat."

Sheldon "Do you know that Christine Devone is engaged to your son?" He shot the question, precipitately.

"The hussy!" she snorted. "Darned little gold-digger is what she is. What she didn't wangle out of a Beckmann, wasn't to be wangled. Just let me catch her marrying my son. Allen!" She stabbed viciously at the binnacle.

Sheldon: "Then you had met her before-" he ventured cautiously.

Mrs. Jason: Never saw the hussy before in my life," she snapped irritably. "I don't believe she was shanghaied."

Sheldon mentioned in a faint voice. 'I don't know what to believe." She scowled ominously.

"But you must have a theory. Won't you tell me what it is?" He had been leading up to his question. Now he wondered if she would express her real opinion. Or, if she would allow her prejudice against Christine Devone to sway her?

Sheldon: "It was a plot to kill Sidney and get his money,"

She thundered. "I don't know whether you are on the level, or not. Maybe I should keep my fool mouth shut."

'Under the circumstances, Mrs. Jason," he began tactfully. "I have as much right to suspect members of your party, as any of you have to suspect me. I don't intend to sit idle and let anyone arrest me for something that I had no hand in. And as I told you before I am as anxious to clear this thing up, as you are. Any help that you can give me will be greatly appreciated."

"I don't know how to go about detecting murderers," she sighed "But if you mean what you say, young man, I'm with you."

Sheldon: "Who do you think wanted Mr. Beckmann's money bad enough to kill him? You must know the contents of his will."

Mrs. Jason: "If you were to receive a million dollars. Why shouldn't I think that the four of you sneaked on board when you found out that I was taking Sidney on a cruise for his health. I bought the Golden Eagle especially for this trip. Sidney was working too hard. I went in to see him one day, and found him in an almost complete state of collapse. Allen was a manager of his uptown office, and he suggested that I bid in on the Golden Eagle. Allen's father originally owned it—my former husband. Allen inherited it, and then lost it thru bad business and gambling.

The people who bought it at that time had to give it up. I bought it. That was last May. I tried to persuade my brother then. But he couldn't see it. He had planned a vacation up in the Adirondacks last year. A lot of good that did him. He came back worse off than ever. So, then Allen thought of China and the Hawaiian Islands. He had been there in 1924 just before his father died. They had discovered some good contracts in Shanghai and there. Allen thinks it may be a large deposit. He told my brother about it.

Poor Sidney never thought Allen had an ounce of business ability. He scoffed at the idea. But I felt that this was the one thing Allen knew all about. He'd been talking about it for years. So, I coaxed Sidney into going. It was Allen's one chance to put himself in solid with the old man. Sidney had to have Philip Dodge along. He never could be satisfied unless he was fiddling with papers. "There, I've told you all our plans. Maybe you knew them before." Her eyes glinted with suppressed agitation.

Sheldon: "I knew nothing of your plans, Mrs. Jason," he said earnestly. "As a matter of fact, Mr. Beckmann never mentioned either your name, or your son to me. He came to the race track in Shanghai a few days ago but he said nothing about any plans for a cruise."

Mrs. Jason: "How did you know that my son was engaged to that hussy?" she asked abruptly.

While Sheldon was thinking up an answer that would not involve an admission that he had rifled Allen's desk, a hoarse voice bellowed: "Hey, Sheldon—" and McClearn bounded up onto the bridge.

Sheldon was startled at the man's appearance. He looked ghastly and perspiration gleamed on his forehead. There has been another murder the mate—"

Mrs. Jason gasped: "Who—Who?" hysterically, and sank onto a bench, her face chalk white with terror.

"The mate," McClearn spluttered. "I was down below talking to the engineer, Mike. One of the crew came bursting in, shouting in his heathenish lingo, and Mike let out a yip and dashed from the room. I ran after him and there was the mate—Nichols, Mike called him, he sat sprawled on the stairway—"

Sheldon noticed that McClearn was clutching something that looked like a tube of shaving cream or tooth paste in his right hand. He interrupted to ask: “What’s in that tube?”

McClearn unscrewed the top, and squeezed the tube. “See how it sparkles?” The tube was labeled—Antiseptic Toothpaste. Mrs. Jason sniffed at it, as she peered over Sheldon’s shoulders. Tiny specks glittered through the round, smooth surface of the oozing cream.

“What is it?” Sheldon asked.

“Powdered glass. I helped Mike carry the mate to his quarters. After we laid him on the bed, *1 went into the bathroom to wash my hands. This was lying on the floor. I stepped on it—the top came off and some of the stuff oozed out. It pricked my fingers as I picked it up.”

“Well?” “Nichols had brushed his teeth with it. I examined his toothbrush.”

“The paste would have tasted gritty, and he would have spit it out,” Sheldon argued.

McClearn: “I know that—but I have my own theory.” He put the cap back on, and tucked the tube in a pocket of his coat and looked wise. “You think there may have been other tubes of tooth paste that contained glass?

That there is something else in the cream beside glass?" Sheldon questioned-

McClearn: "Never mind what I think now. This little tube gets itself analyzed as soon as possible."

Mrs. Jason sighed, wearily. "Did you notify Philip Dodge?"

McClearn: "Didn't think of it.

Chapter 15

"You had no right to move the body without telling Dodge," She blustered. "He's, my lawyer. I put him in charge. Go find him and bring him up here at once. Wait a minute— McClearn had started to descend the stairway. He turned back and faced her. "You lied," she clipped briskly. "That engineer can't speak a word of English."

McClearn: "In a pig's neck—he can't speak English. So could Nichols the mate, and so could Captain Mason." He slammed back and motioned Sheldon to follow him. Allen has escaped," he said, as they reached the deck. "I went directly to your room, and there was no one there. Guess he was too much for West."

"I wonder if West was to be trusted?" Sheldon mused.

As McClearn and Sheldon reached the door of the latter's room, they heard the clumping of heavy feet moving about within the room. McClearn pulled open the door. "Oh, it's you." There was a note of relief in his voice. Sheldon, over McClearn's shoulder saw a rough looking man in a blue denim work-suit.

"This is Mike, the engineer," McClearn explained to Sheldon, and queried: "What are you doing in here?"

Mike: "I been looking at the tooth paste in all the rooms." He held up a tube found in Sheldon's bathroom. "There must be something to that idea of yours. There ain't no gritty stuff in this. But—look at these." He took two tubes from a coat pocket removed the caps and squeezed the tubes. Tiny flecks glittered through the cream, as from the tube McClearn had exhibited.

"Where did you pick those up?" McClearn cried. "One in Cap's quarters, and t'other in Mr. Beckmann's bathroom."

"How many rooms have you been in?" Sheldon asked.

"All of 'em 'cept Mr. Dodge's. He was asleep, so I didn't want him to wake up and catch me fumbling' 'round. I got the bunch of keys from Cap's room."

Sheldon asked: "Did you say that you examined the toothbrush in the mate's quarters?"

McClearn nodded. "Want to look at it?" They went up a narrow flight of steps, and entered a room that looked out on the quarterdeck. The blinds were drawn, and as the engineer flicked on the light Sheldon glanced at the still figure on the bed. The features were drawn, as though death had come in the midst of intense agony. But there was something vaguely familiar about the face. He stared, fascinated.

A man reeling drunkenly, with a chair poised ready to hurl, whirled dizzily into his subconscious vision. This man who had called himself Nichols had been in Shanghai on the previous evening. Sheldon knew, now, how and by whom he had been shanghaied. He moved blindly after the others into the bathroom.

McClearn was holding the toothbrush. He noted that it was still a little damp, and that shiny specks glinted among the bristles. He was wondering who had hired Nichols to slam him over the head, and bring him aboard the Golden Eagle? The engineer was busily searching a medicine cabinet.

McClearn said, “What are you looking for?”

“The confounded thallium',” Mike responded, and continued to push bottles and pill boxes back and forth.

“Whatever that is,” mumbled McClearn.

“It’s an herb the Māori’s use for cuts and bruises. It’s also a deadly poison that they kill people with. It’s tasteless, and it might have been mixed in with the glass in the toothpaste,” he muttered, excitedly. “Nichols always kept’ it here for accidents.”

“Couldn’t it have been put in the food?” Sheldon asked. “Anybody would taste glass in toothpaste.”

Mike: “Not with thallium's high toxicity,” he grunted, “and the thallium' compound is missing.” The way I figure is, it’s less likely to 'be noticed in the toothpaste.

Funny, whoever did it forgot to collect the tubes of them in other rooms.” McClearn said, nodding wisely. “I, read a story once about Māori’s mixing that poison stuff with powdered glass—”

“Who do you think did it?” Sheldon asked. “Cartier, of course. Let’s go find him.”

They left the engineer pawing among the bottles in the medicine cabinet. “We forgot to send Dodge up to Mrs. Jason,” Sheldon reminded, when they were back on deck.

McClearn:“Let her wait. I want to tell you what this engineer guy told me. That heathen language they speak is Polynesian. Allen gave orders to the Captain that the officers were to speak nothing else. The crew can’t. The Captain told him early last evening that there were to be three men put on board, and he gave Mike the suitcases, and told him which room to put them in. Nichols had some of the crew on shore all evening until midnight. They brought us on then. Cartier came aboard early, then left and came back just before they put up steam, with a girl and a suitcase— and the girl was conscious. Mike saw them come aboard —” He paused, waiting for a gesture' of surprise.

Sheldon said drily: “I thought as much.”

“Yes —you did,” McClearn scoffed J “I suppose you knew also that the Captain was mad as blazes about the whole thing and wanted to resign?”!

“My suspicions of Christine Devone! were aroused late this afternoon. I’ll tell you sometime.

Sheldon: “Go on.”

“He tried to interfere with Allen about the girl, and they had an argument. After the Captain was found dead the mate began to talk about mutiny unless more money was forthcoming. He wouldn't tell Mike who he was going to demand this money from. Although he promised to if, he didn't get the money.

Evidently, he didn't get the money—but what in the deuce did he want to go brush his teeth for?" "I tell you that tooth brushing episode is out. If that stuff that the mate mentioned is a deadly poison, it! could have been put in food. The mate was found dead shortly after dinner." "But Mr. Beckmann and the Captain died early this morning—before breakfast." "They had something to drink late last night. Come along, I want to send Dodge up to Mrs. Jason."

They pounded on the door of Room I. After a moment, a sleepy voice said: "Come in." "What is it?" Dodge demanded curtly, as McClearn snapped on the light He was stretched out on the bed, half dressed, and seemed to be very sleepy. He blinked as Sheldon entered, and sat up. "Who let you out?''

"Lucky somebody did," McClearn returned obliquely. "The mate has been killed. And Mrs. Jason wants you up on the bridge." "The mate?" He spluttered and shook his head with a bewildered gesture. "And me lying here asleep. What happened?" McClearn told him briefly, omitting details regarding the toothpaste and the poison. Dodge put on his coat and stumbled out of the room,

He was careful, however, to wait until McClearn and Sheldon emerged, so that he could lock the door. As he rushed ahead McClearn said: "Maybe we'll find Allen in Room J."

Sheldon knocked on the door of Room J. There was no sound from within. McClearn looked into the lounge and came back to Sheldon. "Looks as though we'd lost the girl as well as Allen. Where do you suppose West went to?"

They walked around the deck to Room E. The door was locked, but the window was wide open, curtains fluttering in the wind. Sheldon stuck his head in the window and called There was no one there. They went below, and met Mike in the passage, told him about the three who were missing. He conducted them through every passage and room below. There was no one there.

"Maybe West had a tussle with Allen, and they fell overboard," McClearn suggested. "What about the girl?" "Maybe jumped in to save Allen.?"

"May as well try the bridge. They may be up there." Sheldon said, and, had one foot on the stairway when a feeble cry that seemed to come from the direction of the bow caught their ears. McClearn raced down to the fore deck. Several of the running-lights ' were out, and those that remained cast faint rays, and left part of the fore deck in shadow.

"Over here," whimpered a voice. "He threw me over the rail."

Sheldon walked a few paces, and then saw the little jockey crumpled up against one of the ventilators "What happened?" he asked as he started to lift him.

"Ouch! It's my left leg. I think it's busted," West groaned.

"Let's get him to his room before we do any talking," McClearn advised. They carried him to Room E and laid him on the bed. McClearn examined the leg. Saw that it was badly bruised and bleeding, but not broken. Sheldon helped him tear up a sheet and bandage it. West said between groans. "He struggled out of that rope. I couldn't stop him, so I thought I'd go looking' for you. He caught up with me and near choked me. Then he threw me over the rail. Gee! I thought I was going' in the ocean. I guess I must have' been so scared that I fainted, even though I didn't land in the ocean. I yelled fer you fellows, but I guess you couldn't hear me."

"We were looking for you," Sheldon assured him. Ten minutes later the engineer startled all three of them by walking into the room without knocking. "I heard voices," he explained, "and I've seen a light in here. Thought it might be you two. What's the matter with this guy?"

McClearn told him and added: "What's on your mind?"

"I'm gonna take the Golden Eagle into some port tonight, an' I want your help," he stated grimly. "Mrs. Jason seems to have gone astray because she lost the sextant," Sheldon began.

Mike: "Lost—me eye! There's some scheme afoot to lose all of us. Maybe I'm the next one slated to die fer knowing' too much. I been doing' some heavy thinking.' And when I see that gal spying around the kitchen, I decided it was time to act."

“You found Miss Devone?” Sheldon asked. “Whatever her name is. You know, Mr. McClearn. I don’t know as I think so much of that toothpaste idea, even if it has glass in it. Thallium could be stuck in the food a whole lot easier.

That toothpaste would be a lot of work. And when I see that girl a- snooping’ I think to myself —she’s after me this time. She musta’ been hiding’ down there when the three of us went through a while ago. She won’t be fixing’ any more food. I fixed her all right—”

“What did you do?” the jockey asked, round-eyed and excited.

Mike: “Locked her up—kicking’ an’ screaming.’ And now I want you boys to come up on the bridge with me and the three of us take charge.”

"What about the crew?” Sheldon 1 asked.

Mike: “I helped train that crew. They’ll take orders from me an’ like it. Cartier is up there now with his mother and the lawyer. It’s a suitable time to bust things up.”

“What about me?” West asked hectically, and sat up, forgetting the pain in his leg.

Mike: “Better stay where you are, young feller. It’s likely to get rough up there.

Chapter 16

"What's your plan?" Sheldon interrogated.

Mike: "I got rope enough to tie 'em up. Then I'll take the bridge—l got men that can tend to things below. You two can carry the three of 'em down one at a time and lock 'em up. If they raise a fuss, I'll call some of the Māori to help us. I ain't gonna' stall around here, in midocean waiting' to be killed."

"Mrs. Jason is the owner," Sheldon reminded him. "I think she is a reasonable sort of woman. Suppose you talk with her before you start anything?"

"Reasonable, huh!" he exploded. "In the face of three murders, she put out to sea as fast as she can."

"Come on," McClearn urged. "Mike's right. Give me a length of that rope,' Mike, and I'll lead the attack. We'll! creep in on them. Are you sure Cartier is there?"

"Yep!" Mike nodded, "and it sounded like the three of 'em was all set fer a squabble among themselves."

They left West's room. Mike picked up a coil of rope, which he had left outside the door. Cut it into six lengths and divided it among his companions. McClearn—walking on tip-toe—was in the midst of the three on the bridge before the other two reached the top step. He was holding the rope gripped in both hands behind him. There was a wicked gleam in his eye.

"What do you want?" Dodge asked sourly.

Mike: "I came for Allen," he grinned and made a lunge for that young man, grappled with him. beat him over the face and head with the rope stunned him. Dodge clapped his hands excitedly and Mrs. Jason screamed: "This is: mutiny!"

Sheldon caught hold of her hands! and held them firmly in his grasp, 1 said in an undertone: "Keep cool. I'll see you through." Three burly Māori appeared in the doorway. Mike rapped out orders in Polynesian. Dodge attempted to say something, but the engineer clapped a rude hand over his mouth. The Māori's grinned and muttered imprecations that sounded joyful, as two of them seized the squirming Allen and trundled him down the stairway. Mike motioned the third man to assist McClearn with Dodge, and gave Sheldon a bunch of keys. As Sheldon released Mrs. Jason, Mike seized her, pinioned her elbows from behind and tied her hands.

"Go easy," Sheldon warned him "I'll be back in a minute."

"Say—what do you think you are doing?" she bellowed frantically.

"I'm going to take the Golden Eagle to port," Mike growled, "an' it won't do you no good to scream lady." Echoes of her harsh voice reached Sheldon as he closed the door of Room I, after

McClearn and the Māori had slid their prisoner onto the bed. He found a key that fitted, turned it in the lock and went along the deck to Room G.

"You'll pay plenty for this," Allen threatened, as Sheldon looked in on him. "You stole some papers from me, too, and—"

"I'll be seeing you," Sheldon grinned, and slammed the door and locked it.

Back on the bridge Mike was arguing with Mrs. Jason. "Claims she couldn't find the sextant," Mike snorted, as Sheldon and McClearn came up. "Here it is, tucked under this cabinet. Been here all the time, I guess. Take her away boys." He tossed off a jumble of words to the Māori's. They scrambled speedily down the stairs.

"The sextant was not under that cabinet," Mrs. Jason retorted in an ugly tone, "unless you put it there yourself. God knows, I'm just as anxious as you are to get to Hawaii. "We're a long way from Hawaii," Mike growled.

"Suppose we talk things over with Mrs. Jason?" Sheldon intervened.

"We might be able to come to terms." Mrs. Jason suggested, and focused her attention upon Mike. "You're the engineer, aren't you?"

Mike said: "Yep!" shortly.

"The Captain and the mate were your friends and you're seeing red because they were killed. I don't blame you. I feel the same way about my brother. Whoever put that sextant under the cabinet—it wasn't me. I have an idea that there is someone on board the Golden Eagle who does not want us to get to Hawaii in a hurry. The someone who threw the bodies of Sidney Beckmann and Captain Mason overboard so as the poison, or whatever it was that killed them, would not be detected. I hope you are guarding the body of the mate?"

"I got a man outside the door," Mike told her gruffly.

Mrs. Jason: "Just the same you are going to be locked up." "How much money do you want? And your freedom after we reach port, to let me stay free?" she countered shrewdly.

Mike hesitated: "I don't know that money can buy me."

"Five hundred dollars might come in handy," she suggested

He laughed hoarsely. "It might not be worth it."

"Make her sign a statement that she will work under your command and give you a check for 20 thousand," McClearn said, brazenly.

She glared furiously at McClearn and said:

"Look here, engineer, I understood that none of the officers on the Golden Eagle could speak a word of English. Who gave you orders to assume ignorance of the English language?"

"The Captain."

Mrs. Jason: "Who gave him orders?"

"I'm not supposed to know," he leered.

"Humph! Looks like Allen was completely under the thumb of that hussy. You men have been on the Golden Eagle since it was built, haven't you? Worked for Allen's father, didn't you? So it was Allen who told you not to speak English in front of me. He remembered that I never would go off on the Golden Eagle in the old days, so I wouldn't be likely to know any of its officers or crew." She looked at Mike, but he maintained a glum silence. "Just wait until I get hold of him! Dragging my good name into the dirt like this, with murder, and that terrible woman. Where is she anyway?"

McClearn: "Locked up. If you want to know, I caught her snooping 'round the galley. I figured she was fixing' to dope up some food and that I would be the next to be rubbed out, for knowing' too much."

Mrs. Jason began to manipulate the engine-room telegraph.

"Bring Allen up here," she commanded.

"Not a chance," Mike snickered.

"I'll give you a check for 20 thousand, and we'll see this thing through together." She thumped on a shelf with her fist to emphasize the offer. "

Take it," McClearn urged. "There'll be three of us to see that you get it cashed, and we'll take a chance on raking Allen over the coals up here." "

How much do you want as a rake off?" the engineer squinted suspiciously.

McClearn said, "Not a cent. I can't navigate the damn boat. Neither can Sheldon. That's your pay for getting us back to earth and the authorities. It will be worth it." He glanced at Sheldon for confirmation.

Sheldon murmured: "Good idea!"

Chapter 17

Allen was carried up to the bridge protesting vigorously. "What did you mean by bringing that hussy on board here?" his mother fired, after she had listened to the engineer's story of the sequence of events as he knew them.

"I thought it would be a good chance for you to get acquainted with her. You'd have learned how nice she is, and you and Uncle both would have approved of the marriage. If only these beastly murders hadn't happened," he whined dismally.

"Pshaw!" Mrs. Jason hissed furiously. "You brought that hussy on. board here to poison us all "

"Now, mother. Christine wouldn't poison a rat. She's not the type. And as for your brother, you knew she worshipped him. She always tried to make me understand him."

He was pleading the best he knew how, oblivious of the three men who were listening.

"What was she doing spying around my galley?" Mrs. Jason insisted tenaciously.

Allen puckered his eyebrows and offered: "I don't know what she was doing in the kitchen unless she was looking for evidence. That was eleven of course. She said something about examining the food. She thought Uncle had eaten something.

She talked with me about it. Why the poor girl was heartbroken over Uncle's death."

He was beginning to be incoherent in his anxiety over Christine Devone.

"Heartbroken to the tune of a million dollars." Mrs. Jason pursed her lips and snickered with an ugly sound. "I suppose you think you can marry her and go through that million just like you squandered the three million your father left you. Maybe you had it planned that I was the next to go. so you could fling my money to the four winds," she accused scathingly.

Allen wiggled uncomfortably. "There's no use in suspecting either Christine or me of murder. What about these other people?'

Mrs. Jason: "Never mind the other people. It's time now for you to tell your story. They've told theirs."

Allen: "Where is Christine?"

"Locked up. and she stays there." Mrs. Jason snorted. " Never mind her for the moment. I want to know why you demanded that officers of the Golden Eagle deceive me into thinking that they did not understand English, or speak it?" She faced him resolutely.

Allen's face reddened. He coughed, looked worried, and was silent.

"Well!" McClearn prodded him. "What was the trick?"

Allen: "It was suggested to me this matter of having the

officers speak only Polynesian by a master mind over which I have no control."

"That's a lie." McClearn sneered.

Mrs. Jason: "To think that I'd live to see the day I find my only son a murderer." Mrs. Jason moaned.

“I am not a murder." he protested defiantly. "The question is, who persuaded you to command the officers of the Golden Eagle to speak only Polynesian?" Sheldon put in, coldly.

"Er ---"

McClearn poked him in the ribs.

"There was a master mind but Er… " he stumbled in his speech, and adjusted his glasses nervously.

"But, what?" McClearn prodded him again.

"Dodge " he began weakly.

"That's another lie," his mother snarled. "Dodge had nothing to do with it. Be a man for once in your life and tell your own story”

Allen strained at the cords on his wrists, every nerve tense. "I'm not taking the blame for what I didn't I do." he groaned. "I tell you Philip had some axe to grind. It was his idea to shanghai these two men and the jockey. I thought at first that: he knew them and wanted to play a joke. It was from his talk about getting these men aboard and play- in? a joke on them that I got the idea of having Christine believe that she was shanghaied, also."

"Did he give any reason for wanting to play a joke on us?" Sheldon asked stiffly.

Allen shook his head. "The master mind must have given him orders," he said weakly.

"It's that hussy. Christine Devone who's the master mind." Mrs. Jason contended viciously. "I'd like to wring her neck."

"Do you mind if I go and talk with Dodge alone?" Sheldon asked.

'Go ahead." Mrs. Jason agreed. "Ask him what he thinks of that she-cat."

"Are we going to sit up all night?" McClearn yawned. "It's nearly two o'clock."

"We're going to sit up, son, and ' I'm going to make port by daylight," Mike said stubbornly.

Sheldon went directly to Room I. He found Dodge struggling with the cords on his wrist with one hand almost free. "Did you come to untie these damn knots?" he asked as Sheldon entered the room and sat down.

"No. I came to tell you that Allen has confessed," Sheldon said coldly, and eyed the men before him with slow deliberation.

"To what?" Dodge responded! tersely, and looked unconcerned.

"To everything including the identity to the master mind."

There was an interval of silence. "Allen always was a weakling,"

Dodge sneered at length. "May I ask who the master mind is?" Sheldon did not answer. He was looking at a sheet of paper on the desk beside him. The paper was covered with figures and notations, He picked it up. "Put that down," Dodge snapped irritably, and tried to seize the paper. But in his attempt to stand up. the rope around his; ankle hindered him, and he fell back onto the bed. The figures Sheldon noted, seemed to represent assorted items expended for clothing. It looked suspiciously; like an account of the clothing contained in the suitcases purchased: for himself and McClearn and West.

"You're a fool!" Dodge hissed.; "if you pay any attention to Allen and his talk about a master mind. ' Haven't you ever heard that is a stock phrase?"

Sheldon ignored him. He had found another paper that looked interesting. It was a roughly drawn plan of a house, garage, and garden, with the estimated cost figured on, the margin. It looked like an expensive proposition. Sheldon wondered if Dodge was married. And the next moment came upon a small photograph of Mrs. Jason autographed "Lovingly yours. Mathilda." He dropped "the photograph and clothing estimate into a side pocket of his coat.

Dodge was watching him narrowly.

Sheldon turned upon him abruptly. "Where did you learn Polynesian, Dodge?" Reo Māori, French Polynesia?" The answer was clear after listening to crew outside.

"You were Anthony Cartier's attorney." Sheldon was guessing. "Well?" "You have known Mrs. Jason for years." he was still guessing, and he noticed that Dodge seemed to be the heard the sound of muffled, lagging footsteps on the deck. And the next moment a face appeared at the window. West's face. He was grinning and motioning for Sheldon to open the door. Sheldon called: "Come in," and West limped across the threshold and slumped into the nearest chair eyes bulging with excitement.

"Will you go let Christine out?" he cried. "I called up the stairs to the bridge, but nobody heard me an' I couldn't make the grade, so I; thought I'd try to see if anyone was down here."!

"What do you want Christine out ' for?" Sheldon asked, puzzled. '

West: "She's found something. She found a bottle of poison and some ground glass in the kitchen, some concentrated lemon juice with; the stuff in it."

Sheldon: "How do you know?"

"Me, I got lonesome an' went out an' looked at her through the window. She motioned that she had something' to say, so I busted the glass in the window, an' she told me about finding' the stuff. She'd just packed it into a cupboard when the engineer caught her. She thinks he done the murders.

Sheldon: What motive could he have had?"

West: "I don't know. Maybe he wanted the schooner for himself."

Dodge said sardonically: "If Allen confessed, he must have then implicated the girl. She came on board with him."

Sheldon ignored this remark, and said to West: "Think you can hobble back and unlock the door, if I give you the key?" He was not quite sure that he trusted the little jockey. He had left him alone with Allen, whose hands and feet had been tied, and Allen had escaped. He was taking no chances with Dodge. "Your plans miscarried," he told Dodge as West left. He was playing a hunch, and was uncertain how to play it. Dodge was a lawyer, and knew how to answer questions.

My plans? Dodge queried archly.

"Anthony Cartier died in a mysterious manner on board this yacht in 1923. You were traveling along with him and Allen at the time." he pursued doggedly with his hunch.

"If you have any questions that you would like to ask me. I

wish you would ask them, and stop telling fairy tales." Dodge s voice was calm, tut perspiration gleamed on his forehead and an anxious scowl deepened the lines in his face.

Christine Devone opened the door and stepped across the threshold. What's he trussed up for?" she asked lightly.

Because I want him that way, Sheldon returned coldly.

If you want to know who the murderer is, it's that tough engineer. The way he manhandled me was nobody's business." she blustered, and perched on the edge of the table.

"He had no motive," Sheldon pointed out. "He had a grudge, she snapped back.

An army of people seemed to be scurrying along the deck, and the door of Room I was flung back by Mrs. Jason. Fury blazed in her eyes, 'and she was shaking as she hurled herself into the room and shook a fist in Dodge s face. Allen and McClearn stood framed in the doorway.

"You liar!" she shrieked. "I've just heard the story from Allen and the engineer of how Anthony Cartier was murdered. How you learned a trick from the natives of a Chinese district to grind powdered glass with some heathen poison and stuffing it into tubes of toothpaste. Just two licks of the brush, Allen says, and the stuff takes effect. Nothing was done about Anthony Cartier's murder. Allen, the big coward, was afraid of the 'master mind. Well, this time the 'master mind' is going to burn.

Huh! It was you who advised Allen how to invest the money his father left him. It was you who turned my brother against Allen. It was you abducted the inheritors. Shanghaied 'em because Sidney left them million dollars apiece in his will. Allen was just a love-sick sap, bluffed by a lot of big talk about a 'master mind. Guess you thought you'd kill all four of these dupes along with my brother. Then, as executor, you'd break the will and the money would all come to me, end you'd marry me and invest it. Bah!.'

"The Captain and the mate knew too much, and I'll wager that you had some more tubes of toothpaste fixed up to pass around. You had the bodies thrown overboard. The natives have confessed to that. Thought you were safe, didn't you? You're just a big noise, and your "master mind" is as crooked as a dog's hind leg.

Thought you could play trick on me by hiding the extant back of that cabinet. Maybe you were fool enough to think that we couldn't make port without it " her voice trailed to a husky whisper of exhaustion.

Dodge said coldly: "May I remind you that I was deathly seasick at the time both Mr. Beckmann and Captain Mason met their death, and that I was sound asleep when the man was found dead."

"Not such a good alibi when you figure that it takes from thirty minutes to an hour for the person to die from that mixture. And a person usually brushes his teeth at their own discretion, "McClearn said tartly.

"I found the bottle of poison and some powdered glass in the kitchen and some of the stuff was mixed up in lemon juice. I'm sure" Christine said "That's the way it was dissolved"

Allen just look up sheepishly.

Sheldon motioned to Grey Ebbhart. "Grey here is a professional reporter, and everything has been recorded. Evelyn had done nicely to sketch the crime scenes, the layout of the yacht and passageways. Mac even did a couple tests to time events."

"I first thought the engineer" Christine began, and then lost her voice as Mrs. Jason leveled sharp eyes upon her.

"You want to marry Allen'" she exclaimed brusquely. "I guess Sidney Beckmann must have thought you were all right, or he wouldn't have left you a million." Allen entered the room and wrapped an arm about Christine's' waist. She smiled up into his eyes.

Evelyn and Grey Ebbhart were hand in hand in the corner of the lounge and a happy couple. Greys story of this ordeal and Evelyn sketches would probably fill the AP and appear in papers worldwide.

Mrs. Jason was not totally pleased with this arrangement; however, she had grown very tired of her chaperone role. Young girls over eighteen are hard to manage under a normal household.

Mrs. Jason turned away. "Sheldon!" she barked "you're in charge here. You and McClearn guard this man until we dock."

“What’ll I do?” the jockey said whimsically.

“By the grace of god and maybe some help from Sgt. McClearn I have hopes of making you into a real horseman.” I believe the Army will take a couple of weeks to get all the information they need to insure Lt. Sheldon regains his position on the polo team.

She stormed out of the room. “I have to contact Edward in Shanghai to insure our China affairs are in decent shape. I will be expected to handle most of Beckmann estate and there is quite a debt to be paid before I can catch some decent sleep.”

At 7 o’clock that morning the SS Golden Eagle tied up at the Honolulu dock. Half an hour later the police arrested Philip Dodge and charged him with first-degree murder.

Mrs. Cartier-Jason had torn up the $20,000 check that the engineer handed back to her and presented him with the papers and sea logs of the yacht. “The SS Golden Eagle is lovely, but she cast a shadow on my family and bewitched all aboard,” she gladly poised for photos and chatted with reporters who came on board with the police.

"Our sea adventure will be gladly left far behind us. It is time to get back on track. All this will be explained in a telegraph to the Army in China." Mrs. Cartier-Jason guaranteed her story would be heard and the publicity would help restore a promising military career.

Dick McClearn and James Sheldon had one burning ambition: to play polo with Tommy Hitchcock, the greatest player the sport had ever seen. He was a 10-goal phenomenon who could do anything on the field. He had led the U.S. team to triumph in the International Polo Cup and the Westchester Cup, with other brilliant players like Pete Bostwick, Jock Whitney and Gerald Balding by his side.

Sheldon's final comments were: "We wanted to be part of that team, to wear the same colors and share the same glory. But to do that, we need to work hard on our own game. We need more practice, more experience, and a fine string of horses. We radioed for the support and guidance of our commanding officer - a talented polo player himself. The experience in Shanghai would secure a five-goal handicap and pave the way to becoming a professional player. This sea journey had proven our character and would insure the next assignments and more respect on the polo field. An element of the most prominent in society now know of our honesty, skills, passion, and dedication."

About the Author

Richard D. Colbert is an Educator, Genealogist, and Writer. He graduated with a degree in Sociology from Excelsior College in New York and completed his Master's Degree in Education at Boston University. He is currently a Secondary School teacher and educator in Washington State.

His story line reflects research efforts spanning multiple archives, including newspapers, media data, and on-site sessions at the Congressional Library and Pictorial Archives in Washington, D.C. Currently the focus is to offer enjoyment with fictional novels rich in historical events and of interest to those who desire adventure, service to humanity, and self-fulfillment.

Richard D. Colbert believes that learning never stops, and life always has lessons to teach us; thus, sharing social history and events have become a passion.

Made in the USA
Las Vegas, NV
07 August 2023

75760401R00095